HOLIDAY BLUES

HOLIDAY BLUES

A Sweet Holiday Romance

SARA BREAKER

Zeta Indie Publishing

Contents

I

Stuck

I turned up the music from my beat-up portable radio playing the Chipmunks version of "Deck the Halls."

Mostly to drown out my roommate Wanda's off-key singing in the shower.

So far this year, the only thing reminiscent of the season were the white flakes of snow that had been falling outside for the last twenty-four hours.

It was Christmas Day. But with everything snowed in, it had been impossible to go home to California for the holidays.

I stared out the window of our college housing. The front walk was already covered and I cringed at the forethought of tomorrow's shoveling.

A picture print Mom and Dad had sent sat on the desk beside my narrow, still-unmade bed.

"See you soon! Love you, Hon! - Mom and Dad" was stickered

inset of a photo capture of our living room back home having been enthusiastically decorated for the holidays.

My mom usually went hard-out, always putting little gold-lined red bows on literally everything.

This year's motif was teddy bears. Not only was the Christmas tree adorned with all kinds of these little fluffy toys but Mom had also decided to create a chandelier-type decoration of an assortment of bears. It hung above a dining table that was tidily set with silverware and red candles in gold candlesticks adorned with green wreaths.

I turned to survey my surroundings. In absolute contrast, our room was perhaps not looking so jolly.

Half of mine and Wanda's clothes were strewn on the floor, cabinet doors ajar, tubes of moisturizers and make-up cluttered several surfaces.

Torn gift wrappers, half-open presents, cards, candy canes and noisemakers, streamers, and glittery balloons pushed haphazardly to one side.

Though Wanda had gone through the tiny effort of decorating the little succulent plant she kept on the windowsill with a gold ribbon bow and a smattering of tinsel.

I walked over to sort through some laundry, knowing full well Wanda would need a few more minutes.

It was my first Christmas away from home. I hadn't even been able to go back for Thanksgiving either.

And although the university's Christmas party last night had all the hallmark necessities required to celebrate the season of perpetual hope, spiked fruit punch and all, I couldn't help but still be a bit homesick.

I missed my own bed. I missed my family. And...maybe someone else.

I heaved a huge sigh before finally deciding to yell out, "Wanda! Aren't you done yet? We were supposed to be at The Corner like a half-hour ago."

Wanda floated out of the bathroom in a cloud of mist, drying her shoulder-length red hair with a towel as she hummed "God rest ye merry gentlemen."

She and I had known each other for about two years, ever since my first roommate received a scholarship to an Ivy League school and moved away.

And Wanda Meyers could not have been more different from the quiet, studious girl she had replaced.

Wanda was the kind of person who had already decided that the world was her own private party. Ergo, if there *was* a party, she started it. And if there wasn't one, she was going to start one.

Today was no exception.

Frowning, she cast me a glance, noting the dark cloud over my head. "Dude, you are totally bringing the whole mood down," she chided. "It is *one* holiday."

Obviously, Wanda didn't understand my mope. She usually only went home to Florida for the long summer break, mostly because she didn't feel like bouncing between each of her parent's condos.

She cocked her head to one side. "And what on Earth are you listening to?"

She jumped to flick a switch on my radio and it blasted out the instrumental part of a Jet song and her eyes lit up. "Yes!"

Thumping beats blared out of the little tinny radio, filling our entire room, and Wanda, in her fluffy purple robe, began to dance around, playing air guitar.

After approximately thirty seconds, stamping footsteps came up the stairs.

"Whoops." I glanced up toward the door, already in expectation.

Yvette Molenberg was a junior like us. She had the room below ours and often complained about our "heavy as elephants" footsteps, allegedly distracting her from her all-important "honors-aiming" schoolwork.

This morning, she appeared at the doorway, her mascara-laden gaze already narrowed, hands on the hips of her decidedly hipster button-down brown frock.

Her glare landed on my radio before darting up at me.

Note: Not Wanda. Me.

"De Luca, how many times do I have to tell you, you are not the only—"

Wanda bounced over to Yvette, putting an arm around her shoulders. "Heyy! Good morning, Yvette! How is your lovely self? Make any important emotional breakthroughs lately?"

"Meyers." Yvette made a face as she shrugged her off. "The only breakthrough I'd like to find is one that gags you for life. Now, turn that racket down. Not all of us were born lucky enough to just coast through finals without actually doing the work," she lamented before directly stalking away.

"Thank you, have a nice day!" Wanda called out after her.

I chuckled out my relief. "Thanks." I checked my wristwatch. "She made good time today, considering."

Wanda whacked the radio lightly with her fist to turn it off and rolled her eyes. "What a sourpuss," she remarked as she got changed. "If you ask me, she still hasn't recovered from when you edged her out at that all-state whatever-it-was academic competition you were in last year."

I shrugged as that had indeed been when Yvette had started to become even more antagonistic to me than usual. "I didn't even place! It's not like I was intentionally trying to beat just her."

Wanda simply shook her head, grabbing my arm and her jacket and pulling me out the door. "You can't let that girl walk all over you. I've told you a million times, you need to be a little more self-assured, a little more aggressive. You know, a little more—"

"Like you?"

Wanda laughed as we headed downstairs. "Well, yes, if you prefer to phrase it that way."

I shivered as we stepped outside the two-story duplex. "Brr, check out that sky. I don't think it ever cleared up."

Wanda looked heavenward, kicking up snow with her boot as we walked. "It didn't," she said, now humming "The Little Drummer Boy" as she and I fast-walked down the lane.

I sidestepped a slush puddle, frowning as it was a futile attempt to stop the wetness from seeping its way into my shoes.

One thing I loved about living in California was that it never, ever got this frigid and dreary. Served me right for choosing to study at an East Coast school.

Then again, I'd never had to be stuck at school during winter vacation before.

I recalled a particularly warm memory of being at the

beach quite a few years ago, playing volleyball on the sand, sharing mango smoothies...

I flicked some snowflakes off my nose with yet another disgruntled sigh. "Wanda, what are we going to do for the whole next week?"

"Well..." She tilted her head, gesturing at my sullen face. "We could do all *that*." Then she put up an index finger, her eyes lighting up. "Or—you just follow my lead. When have I ever steered you wrong?"

"Gosh, I'm so scared right now." It wasn't hard to feign another shiver. "Besides, what's school on a holiday anyway aside from a big, giant ghost town?"

And when Wanda replied, it was with a twinkle in her eye. "A paradise with an all-boys dorm where guys who didn't go home either hang out. Of course."

"Meyers, your motivation as always is something to be admired. However, I'm starting to have a theory that only flaky, weird people with family issues stay on campus around the holidays." I emphasized a gesture towards her.

"Come on, Ash. Think about it. Aside from Yvette and a couple of random upper-class flirts, the grazing field has significantly narrowed."

I gave her a measured look. "And what use is that? What kind of guys do you actually know will be around? You know, except for—oh shoot!" I ducked behind Wanda as I glimpsed the familiar back of someone's head by the wooden benches that lined the path.

Wanda turned wide around to see me. "What are you doing?"

"It's Gilbert Lawson." I hunched over, clutching the side of her jacket to cover my face.

She groaned. "Jeez, are you still hiding from that little guy?"

"I'm not hiding."

Wanda rolled her eyes. "Says you in a hoarse whisper as you hide behind my stylish faux mink parka."

"Just—would you just walk faster?" I couldn't help a laugh at the ridiculous situation.

Wanda eyed the group who fortunately seemed deeply involved in their card game on the bench as we skittered past. "Hey, seriously, I'll flash him again if you need another distraction. Just say the word."

My neck was still craned back in caution but my shoulders slacked in relief before I shot Wanda a pointed look. "He's afraid of you, you know that."

"Exactly." She winked. "Aren't you ever so glad to have me around?"

I laughed. "Maybe I should officially hire you to be my bodyguard," I remarked as we arrived at the café.

The Sweet Corner was just outside of campus, a remodeled old diner with a classic jukebox. With the glittery fairy lights, red and green wreaths against the snowy white backdrop, it looked more quaint than usual.

Although the place wasn't as full as it was during the semester and I easily spotted the familiar faces of our friends at the window of the most coveted booth—the one we could never get on a regular school day, the one by the frosted bay windows.

The bells over the door jangled as Wanda and I pushed to come in.

But she had spotted something else too and elbowed me to look over.

It wasn't hard to figure she was referring to the table full of big, towering football jocks at the end of the row.

I made a slow nod. "Ohh, so when you said you had plans for the holiday break, you meant a specific plan. A plan with a name."

Wanda flashed me a grin. "Perhaps the name Doug Taylor."

I made a face. "What? Again? I thought you were done with that whole business last year—remember at Lambda Kappa? When you insisted on buying him at that dumb auction but he spent the night calling you Shonda?"

"What? It was for charity. And Shonda is a beautiful name. Come on, it's all water under the bridge," Wanda dismissed. "Besides, good-looking guys hang out with other good-looking guys." She rushed on, not even taking a breath. "And don't even start with me. There's no harm in looking."

"Sure, tell that to your boyfriend." I stopped to point out, my eyebrows raised, "Oh, yes, that's right. You *have* a boyfriend."

"So?"

"And by the way, so do I."

Wanda narrowed her eyes. "Jason is not your boyfriend. He just happened to be the first guy you'd ever gone out with like when you were five, and then a billion years ago, he moved away."

The mere mention of my guy-that-sort-of-got-away imme-diately sent butterflies to my stomach.

Yeah, that vivid memory of a shared mango smoothie at the beach. Guess who that was with?

Jason Hart was, for all intents and purposes, my childhood sweetheart. We had been inseparable and used to do everything together right through middle school until his family all packed up and PCS'd to Alaska.

We had been keeping in touch all these years and I was more than hopeful that his return would reverse the "got-away" part.

I pursed my lips, snapping back to the present. "Yes. And now he's moving back," I reminded her. "We were even supposed to see each other yesterday. Except now I'm stuck here with you," I remarked with a scoff.

Wanda laughed.

"And what about *Locky*?" I breathily mocked Wanda's pet name for the poor soul she was supposedly going out with.

Wanda dismissed it with a wave of her hand. "Locky schmocky," she said. "He's miles away."

"And just because he's not likely to find out means it's a terrific idea for you to flirt with other guys?"

"I'm so glad you agree."

I rolled my eyes. "I absolutely *do not*. I think you're making a big mistake."

Wanda put her hands on her hips and gave me that look. "How did I ever manage to pick up a friend like you?" She shook her head in disapproval. "You need to learn to be more supportive, Ashleigh."

All I could do was shake my head in mirth. There was really no stopping Hurricane Wanda.

"This will be the best worst vacation you'll ever have," Wanda promised, already bounding across the café. "Trust me!"

2

Friends

"Hey, guys." I nodded my greeting as I reached our booth, giving one of my friends a high-five before taking off my jacket.

"Ashleigh, perfect." Stella Hoffman leaned her elbows on the table to give me an even look. "Would you please give these two ding-dongs a bit of sense?"

"Baby," Pete Rodriguez began, patting her back. "Pastels are coming back. Think what an awesome statement it would make."

"Yeah, we are pretty awesome statement-makers." Spencer, Stella's brother, sat across the booth from them and gave Pete a fist bump. "Remember last Halloween, we even won 'Best Costume' with the Rocky Horror Picture Show bit."

"And just like Halloween, baby, I'm telling you, if you do that again, I'll be pretending not to know you," Stella told Pete, a firm look on her face.

I cast each of them an amused look. "What is going on?"

Stella rolled her eyes. "These two want to 'dress up' at my parents' fancy Boxing Day Gala on Friday night. Can you please remind them how humiliating that freshman mixer was? I was like the third wheel to their 'Dumb and Dumber' comedy act."

I had to laugh at the memory.

Stella gestured to me. "See? Ashleigh agrees with me. If you guys don't care about your reputation, care about mine, please."

Pete made a face. "Come on, Stella. Ashleigh's like the last person you can ask for an opinion on this."

I shot him an almost-already-offended look as I nudged Stella to move over on the booth. "What is that supposed to mean?"

Spencer rolled his eyes, giving me a pointed look. "Are you kidding? You never want to call attention to yourself and you hate confrontations." He tutted with a shake of his head, "You can't fly under the radar forever, Ash."

"Yeah," Pete chimed in. "How many times have you let people cut in front of you in line and you don't even complain? I mean come on, you've never even sent food back at a restaurant even when they've legit made a mistake."

I feigned a retch. I could never quite explain it but the mere thought of having to call someone out and then embarrassing myself if I turned out to be wrong already sent my pulse racing in anxiety.

What if I had just misunderstood and I was making a big deal out of nothing?

Somehow I would always find myself rationalizing in their favor or pretending nothing happened.

"Guys," Stella corrected. "The thing is Ash is just way too nice. She always wants to please everybody." She turned to me. "Admit it. You've been like this since high school."

I shot her a suffering look. "Fine, fine. Make fun of Ashleigh, the doormat. Next time you need someone to help you corral your ant farm back at two in the morning, don't come crawling back to me."

That made Pete laugh.

"The point is," Spencer cut in, banging his fist on the table like a gavel, "while Ash, angel that she is, would never condone something like this, this is the stuff that my blood brother Pete and I were born to do."

"That's it." Stella threw her hands up. "You guys should just never be allowed in the same city, let alone the same party," she complained. "Spencer, this is all your fault. If you had graduated last year and moved to New York, Pete wouldn't be getting all these crazy ideas."

"Oh, so it's my fault now. Mom said she totally understood that I wanted to take some time to try out this Law elective before I put the big company suit on," Spencer explained. "Besides, you're the one who wanted Pete to spend Christmas here instead of going home to Chicago."

"Yeah," Pete interjected. "I'm already spending Christmas with your family. Why can't you just appreciate how devoted a boyfriend I am and also appreciate my fashion sense?"

Spencer and Pete laughed, roughhousing against each other across the booth that Stella just rolled her eyes.

"Ugh. Changing the subject," she said, turning to me. "How's the flight hunting going, Ash?"

Ash frowned. "Well, everything's still grounded. I'm on standby for Sunday evening but it's still up in the air, so to speak."

"Bummer." She pursed her lips, her gaze distracting to a waitress walking past with a tray. "Weren't you supposed to meet up with lover boy Jason again? At long last?"

I threw up my hands. "Exactly! It sucks is what it is."

"Hey, is that that Jason guy who sent you snow from Alaska in a tiny glass bottle or something?" Pete prompted, rapping on the table.

"It was a bottle of water," Spencer couldn't help to add, matter-of-factly.

I swung my arm to try to whack the side of his head but he wove away. "Yeah-huh. He's always been the sweetest."

"He was bossy," Spencer interjected.

"Please don't mind my brother." Stella reached over to whack the side of his head, this time landing it and making him yelp out. "Spencer has no romantic bone in his entire body."

The waitress came around again with another tray, this time stopping beside us to unload several colorful drinks.

"Well hey, since you're stuck here with us this week, why don't you come along to the Gala too?" Stella proposed as she flicked a little packet of cinnamon back and forth between her fingers. "You haven't been to one since we moved from California. Remember how we used to put Mountain Dew in Mom's champagne flutes and pretend it was Cristal?" She gestured carelessly out the door. "I'm sure my parents would love to see you."

I made a face. "Stella, it was okay when we were younger and we could fool around. But we're supposed to be grown-ups now. And these guys will tell you already, I really won't be good with that scene."

Spencer was already nodding in agreement as he stirred his loaded Christmas milkshake with the paper straw.

"Oh, come on," she chided, nudging my shoulder. "It'll be fun. In any case, you should still come earlier and help us with the prep. You're still the only one of us that can work those blasted, complicated multimedia equipment."

I chuckled. "Maybe. I don't know what I'm doing yet on Friday. Wanda said she wanted to do something. Can she come too?"

Stella stopped short and shook her straight black hair out of her eyes, her reply tentative. "Um, maybe."

I gave her a look. "It's been two years, Stella. Are you still sore about Wanda flirting with Pete? You're gonna need to get over that. She didn't know he was your boyfriend."

"Also, Pete performed admirably," Pete himself put in. "Wanda had no effect on Pete whatsoever."

I had to laugh but Stella's face was still somber.

"I'm just sayin', don't let yourself get sucked into her demented world. Too much drama. You'll never escape."

I gave her an *oh-come-on* look. "She's seriously not that bad."

An eruption of cheers burst from across the café and we all looked over.

"Hmm...looks like more drama is afoot. What do you

suppose is going on over there?" Spencer's curious gaze as well as half his upper body had been turned toward the jock table.

I craned my neck to look.

Wanda was having a lively chat with Doug and his friends and someone had produced a sprig of mistletoe.

I wrinkled my nose, already in knowing distaste.

Pete whistled. "Looks like Wanda's not wasting any time. She's like an attack dog with a mark."

"Are we forgetting this is Wanda?" Stella quipped. "I'm surprised she's not already serving eggnog shots from her belly button."

Pete noted the wistful look on Spencer's face and smacked his back. "Sorry, bud. I've told you a million times. Wanda's never going to like you like that. Not unless you build some serious muscles. Or drop your IQ about fifty points," he suggested with a grin since we already all knew he was harboring a not-so-secret crush on Wanda.

"As if." Spencer shrugged him off, his expression while fully incredulous, still unconvincing. "Besides," he went on, giving me a prompting look. "Wanda's already got a boyfriend. She does, right?"

"Supposedly," I replied, reaching over to steal some of the chocolate-covered marshmallows off his drink.

"Hey, hey!" Spencer swatted my arm away. "Stop stealing my marshmallows. Order your own drink, Ash! Every time, seriously?"

That made Stella laugh and she high-fived me even as I stuck my tongue out at him. "So much for 'friendship means sharing.' Save my seat," I bid as I stood up.

I was heading over to the counter when Wanda rushed

over and pulled on my arm, dragging me all the way toward the ladies' room.

"Owowowowow!" I yelped as she closed the door behind us. "What's the big idea?" I demanded.

"You'll never guess what just happened." Her eyes were crazy wild, her voice echoing against the teal tiles, over the music in the bathroom playing Mariah Carey's ever-so-ubiquitous Christmas carol.

"Um, Doug asked you out?" I asked flatly.

Wanda frowned. "Yeah. But you weren't supposed to actually guess. I was supposed to tell you."

I stifled my laughter. "Big deal. So what's with all the secret secrecy? It's not like everybody's not going to find out anyway."

"It's just—don't tell him about Locky, okay?"

"Like he would ask me."

"And don't *tell* Locky."

I stopped short.

I had only met Locky in person twice, maybe picked up the phone a few times whenever he called and Wanda was out.

He seemed like a nice enough person but all I knew about their whirlwind relationship was that it had started when they were both counselors at Camp Morningwater back in Florida.

I had, of course, heard enough of the stories of hot and heavy making out under the full moon, drinking hot cocoa by the campfire, seeing stars in each other's eyes. Leave it to Wanda to only share the really important details.

So I had no idea what else Wanda was looking for outside of her seemingly ideal, long-term relationship.

Especially since Doug, on the other hand, didn't seem to have any more to offer than an impressive athletic record and from what I'd heard, certainly an impressive track record with women too.

But I was more than happy to be proven wrong. Some people *could* be more than their looks.

"Well?" Wanda prompted.

It occurred to me that if I knew Jason was fooling around with someone else, I would most definitely want to know about it.

"I don't know." I fidgeted in my stance.

"Oh, come on, please!" Wanda made a pouty face up at me, clasping her hands together, significantly emphasizing the 'e' in "please."

Honestly, it was really none of my business. And I could already tell what was going to happen. Read: total disaster. This was absolutely going to blow up in her face.

But maybe she needed to learn that lesson on her own. Maybe this was just the kick in the pants Wanda needed to get some sense. No platitudes from anyone else had certainly ever managed to dissuade her from her evil plans anyway.

Besides, she was giving me that pathetic look. *You are my best friend in the whole entire world. Do me this one eensy-weensy-teensy favor.*

And as far as favors went, I did owe Wanda a few. I didn't want to let her down.

I blew out a huge sigh in concession. "Okay, okay."

"Great!" Wanda squealed, her eyes bright as she squeezed my arm.

"So I guess I'm going to be home alone tomorrow night

then, huh?" I prompted as the two of us made our way back to the counter.

She looked at me like I was dense. "You mean tonight?"

Yes. Wanda wasn't wasting any time at all.

3

Locky

I wasn't watching Wanda get ready for her date. I *was* trying to relax in bed and concentrate on reading my book.

But Wanda was buzzing all around our tiny room.

She had already tried on several different outfits, several pairs of shoes, and several different hairstyles, and she wasn't even done yet.

I shot her a bemused look. "I wonder what *Locky* would think of that outfit."

Wanda cast me a flat glance. "Dude, I haven't been on a date in a super long time. I just need to feel that—" She paused, holding up a chiffon blouse to herself, her head tilted with a faraway dreamy look. "That magic again, you know...?"

I wasn't even able to respond as after a split second, her dreamy expression morphed into another frown as she peered into the little mirror hanging on the wardrobe door. "Ash, seriously, next time you go home, you're bringing back a full-length mirror, okay? I'm dying over here!"

I had to laugh, pushing to sit up in bed. "Why don't you just borrow Yvette's downstairs? I hear her room is a regular woman cave."

"What, and turn into the creature from the black lagoon or something?" Wanda made a face. "No thanks. She probably cast some spell on that to make other people look fat or something."

"I'll bet it makes her look better."

When the phone rang, I jumped up to get it. "It's downstairs," I told Wanda, covering the mouthpiece. "Doug's here." I checked my watch. "And he's late."

"I'm later," Wanda said, brushing her hair.

"Thanks, Becca." I put down the phone before giving Wanda another scrutinizing look. "Aren't you even done yet?"

"Ooh, I wonder why someone is so eager to be alone." She shot me a mischievous look. "Maybe someone's expecting a long-distance call from someone."

I was going to refute it but my eager jump when the phone rang again definitely betrayed me. "Yes?" I said as I picked up, my eyes surely wide in anticipation dimming when I recognized the voice on the other end. "Oh, hi, Mom."

Wanda let out a breezy laugh.

I stuck my tongue out at her before responding to my mother. "Fine, I'm fine. Yeah, she's here too. She's just getting ready to go out." I met Wanda's gaze. "Uhh...the library," I fibbed because despite how much it seemed that Wanda could do no wrong in front of my mother (read: giant kiss-ass), there was no need for my mom to know that anybody in this room was going out to see any boys.

Wanda gave me a wink and a thumbs-up. "Hello, Mrs. De Luca!" she called out loud.

"Mom says hi," I whispered.

"I'm going now, Ashleigh." Wanda gave me a spirit-fingers wave as she headed out the door, her voice all melodious, teasing. "Have fun with Yvette."

"See you!" I waved her away. "Stay safe—and shut the door!" I called, lowering the phone for a moment.

Wanda grinned and walked away, leaving the door wide open just to be annoying.

I had to shake my head, walking over just enough to nudge the door with my toe, not caring that it was still an inch ajar. "Yeah mom, I'm still here. Wanda's just stepped out." I fell back on my bed with a sigh. "Yeah Mom, I miss you guys too."

I sort of lost track of time because naturally, there was another party at my house, all my family were there, and Mom just had to give me a blow-by-blow of everything.

Though I had to admit, stories about home were like a soothing balm to my homesickness. Even if Grandpa Jack fell asleep on the couch and was snoring so loud, the dog started barking thinking he was a lawnmower. Or that Cousin Stacy's baby spit up all over the new sheepskin rug. Or that my nephew Tyler almost broke a lamp.

"I know. I'm trying to get a flight so I can at least make New Year's," I said, still sprawled on my bed, already imagining how beautiful the fireworks would be, especially since Jason had agreed to attend my family's New Year's Eve party having missed me at Christmas. "I really hope this weather cooperates."

A loud knock snapped me out of my melancholy.

"Whoops—hang on, Mom." I jumped up, carrying the phone to open the door.

Some guy wearing a distressed black leather jacket with his back to me was standing in the hall.

"Um, can I help you?" I asked uncertainly, trying to peer around him.

He spun around. "Ashleigh!"

My eyes popped out of my head when I met his gaze. "Locky!"

He cringed a little and I had to check myself but he spoke first, "You can call me Lachlan."

My jaw dropped as I cringed myself. "Oh, of course, Lachlan! Um, what are you doing here?"

"I'm here to see Wanda. Is she around?"

"Um, no," I said and changed the subject again. "How did you get upstairs?" I craned my neck out the door in wonder.

"Becca tried to page you but—" He gestured to the phone in my hand. "It was busy."

"Oh." I suddenly remembered that my Mom was still on the line. "Oh! Gosh! Wait a sec." I put my hand up, turning back to the phone. "Mom?" I turned back. "Yeah, I have to go. No, it's just a friend of Wanda's. Yes, I'm fine. See you! Okay, Mom, bye! Love you too."

I tossed the phone onto my bed and turned back to Lachlan, still a bit disoriented. "Ah...did Wanda know you were coming?"

"No," Lachlan replied with a slight frown. "It was kind of a surprise."

"Well, it is," I said with a nod. "She's not here. Uh…" I racked my brain for some brilliance. "She went… to the uh… library." I promptly changed the subject again before that strange note could settle. "Well, you—you look so different. I almost didn't recognize you."

It was true. He seemed to have gotten even taller, he had grown out his crew cut, and the leather jacket was definitely new.

Lachlan bent his head a little, I thought he blushed. "Yeah, well." He shoved his hands in his pockets before giving me a curious look. "Did you say Wanda's at the library?"

Obviously, "Wanda" and "library" were the furthest things to make sense together since peanut butter and banana.

"Yeah," I tried to recover. "I guess she's…turning over a new leaf!"

"Um, okay." Lachlan shrugged.

"So does she know you're here?" I asked, again, stupidly.

His smirk quirked a bit. "You already asked me that."

"Oh. Right." I averted my wide-eyed, slightly panicked gaze and wanting to hit myself over the head. "Well, uh, in any case, like I said Wanda's out."

I discreetly checked the time on the digital clock by my bed. The house curfew was about to kick in and I was hoping Doug and Wanda weren't on their way back yet or they might just run right smack into him. I couldn't stop my own heartbeat from pounding but I willed myself to chill out. It wasn't even *my* problem.

"Uh, so uh...are you just passing through? Going back to Florida soon?"

"No." He shook his head, leaning against the doorway. "I'm staying for a few days."

"Oh, I'm sorry!" I noticed his stance and straightened up. "Do you have to go now?"

Lachlan tilted his head. "Is it okay if I wait? In case Wanda comes back?"

"Okay, well, would you like to—" I stopped short at my gesture into the room as it was currently a Department of Sanitation nightmare and diverted quickly. "—go downstairs and sit down?"

"Sure."

"Give me two minutes." I spun around and shut the door so I could at least get changed into something looking half-human. As I shut the door, I caught sight of myself in the tiny mirror and gasped.

I was a mess! I was wearing a halter top, old sweatpants, and my hair looked worse than the room.

After the shortest two minutes ever, I burst back out the door, hair in a tidy ponytail and I'd thrown on a gray sweater, jeans, and sneakers.

"Hey," I piped up breathlessly, closing the door behind me.

Lachlan raised his eyebrows in acknowledgment. "I guess I really came at a bad time," he noted as we both walked downstairs. "So much for the surprise."

"Well, you surprised me so I wouldn't say it was a total loss."

I led him downstairs to the receiving room in the lobby and gestured for him to sit on the couch with his back to the door in case Wanda and Doug came in.

"Soo..." I started as I slumped into the other armchair. "Did you just get into town? How's it been going?"

He nodded. "Yeah, I'm on Christmas break from school too. I just hitched a ride with a friend—sorry about the late visit." He narrowed his eyes. "Hey, don't you usually go home for Christmas?"

"Oh, yeah, the crazy weather grounded all the flights." I made a face. "So where are you staying? Hotel?"

"No. I'm crashing with another friend. He actually lives near campus," Lachlan relayed, looking around, fidgeting in his seat. "What time did you say Wanda would be back?"

"Oh, I can't...say really," I fibbed. "It could be much later."

"What time do libraries close around here?" Lachlan gave me a curious look.

I pursed my lips, already apprehensive about my white lie. According to Wanda, aside from being a good kisser, Lachlan was also somehow pretty smart and I was sure he was going to find some loophole in my crappy logic in about a minute.

"Oh, uh, you know, she might be at the one that's open all night." I averted my gaze trying to rack my brain.

I was *almost* sure at least one of the libraries on campus was open twenty-four hours, and if Lachlan asked for the specific name, I'd better have it. Otherwise, I would be so busted.

But when I looked at him again, it was obvious Lachlan was as uncomfortable as I felt. Maybe he already knew I was lying to his face. His expression was sullen and I noticed he was avoiding my gaze too.

My shoulders slacked in ridicule of our current situation. I propped my elbow on my knee, leaning over. "Listen," I began. "It'll probably be better if you come back tomorrow.

Or you know, call first," I suggested, trying not to enunciate too hard.

Lachlan narrowed his eyes at me as though trying to measure my meaning, but he didn't press. "You're probably right," he said, starting to stand. "But it's probably better if *she* calls me. Here's my new number." He handed me a piece of paper.

"Right." I stood up myself, pocketing the slip of paper, and gestured toward the door as if it could somehow make him leave faster.

"Thanks, Ashleigh."

"It was good to see you again," I bid, even as I glanced warily outside to make sure the coast was still clear.

He let out a small sigh. "Tell Wanda, I'll drop by again tomorrow morning anyway, would you? And tell her I...really want to see her."

"Of course."

Seeing the downcast look on his face, I couldn't help but feel bad for him. He had come all this way to see his girlfriend whom he missed so much.

Meanwhile, said girlfriend was out with another guy, probably not giving her own boyfriend much thought at all.

It was a good thing Lachlan was preoccupied putting his scarf on just then because as we walked down the front steps, whose fancy-ass sports car must come swerving to a stop to park right by the sidewalk?

That's right.

And oh look, Wanda's stepping out the passenger door.

Uh-oh.

Wide-eyed, my gaze snapped up to Lachlan who was about to casually stroll down the footpath.

Oh, shoot.

"Ow, ow!" I said aloud, feigning a limp and crouching by the steps.

Lachlan turned around, alerted. "What's wrong?"

I glanced up in Wanda's direction hoping she could see exactly what was going on over here before meeting Lachlan's gaze. "Um, ow, I think I...sprained my—my ankle," I said with a grimace, if not from the pain, from the embarrassment of having to do this at all.

I was not a good actress. Inwardly, I was kicking myself. What the heck was Wanda making me have to do? I cursed under my breath in relief when I spotted Wanda leading Doug out back.

Thank goodness.

"Let's get you back inside to sit down." Lachlan's forehead was creased as he took my arm to help me.

"Oh, uh, I think it's fine now." I straightened up in an instant. "Thanks."

"What?" Lachlan shot me a look. "Are you sure?" He surveyed me up and down as if to gauge for himself.

I flushed red in absolute mortification. This was absolutely ridiculous. "Yes. Thanks."

I was so going to kill Wanda.

4

Last Favor

I must have appeared like the ghost of Christmas past bursting through the door.

"What the heck was that all about?" I demanded.

But Wanda was already just as distressed, pacing the floor. "Oh my gosh, what was Locky doing here? What did you tell him? You didn't tell him I was out with Doug, did you?"

I gave her a suffering look as I trudged back to my bed. "Your boyfriend wanted to surprise you. He's on school break too. He misses you sooo much." I paused, wryly. "By the way, how was your date?"

Wanda's eyes widened but this time with excitement as though already having completely forgotten the earlier dilemma altogether. "Oh, it was amazing! Doug can be so romantic..." she trailed off with a sigh.

I blinked hard and barked out my question, "What?"

She jumped, almost looking innocent. "What?"

I groaned. Obviously, when I had stupidly sanctioned her going out with Doug, I had never imagined that I would somehow be caught in the middle of her chaotic Wanda web mess.

"Wanda! What are you going to do about your boyfriend?" I threw my hands up.

Wanda rolled her eyes. "Locky is gone."

I pursed my lips pointedly. "He says he'll come back to see you tomorrow."

"What? He can't!" Wanda backed up a step. "I have another date tomorrow."

"Are you freaking kidding me?"

Wanda's mind had gone off to dreamy dream land again. "Doug wants to take me ice skating at the pond."

I gawked. "Are you serious? What about Lachlan?"

Wanda waved her hand. "You can just tell him I'm at the— library or something."

"I can't! I told him that tonight."

"Then tell him it's a *huge* project," Wanda dismissed with a shrug.

I let out a derisive laugh. "No. *I'm* not going to do anything because *you* are going to tell him."

Wanda finally let out a groan. "Ugh, come on, Ash! I can't deal with this right now. Can't you just please do this one thing for me? I don't want to cancel on Doug tomorrow."

"You are unbelievable." I shook my head. "Are you seriously giving up Lachlan for Doug?"

She made a face. "No! Of course not. I just...I haven't seen him for so long. Do you know how often we've talked these past few months? Hardly ever! And he's just so—blah..."

"Jeez, why don't you just break up with him then?"

Wanda's eyes lit up. "Oh my gosh, you're right. I should just break up with Locky."

My own eyes popped out of their sockets. Of all the insensitive, flippant remarks I could possibly say! "Oh shoot, I didn't mean that!" My stomach churned at the instant recall of how miserable Lachlan had looked earlier and here, I had just gone and possibly whacked the final nail in his coffin.

I hopped over to brace my hands on her shoulders to give her a quick shake. "Wanda, settle down. You're not going to break up with Locky."

She narrowed her eyes at me. "I'm not?"

I shook my head briskly.

Wanda heaved a huge sigh. "Alright, fine. Look, I know it's unfair to keep stringing him along. And I will talk to him, okay? Just not tomorrow. Please?" She gave me that look again, batting her eyelashes. "Friend? Help me out? This is the last time you'll have to cover for me, I promise, and I swear I'll never ask you for anything ever again."

I really wanted them to work everything out and the odds were it definitely wouldn't happen if Wanda stood up Lachlan again tomorrow without even a word.

Someone had to do something.

Ugh. This was so going to come back to bite me, wasn't it?

It was hard to keep glaring at Wanda's pleading expression. I let out a long resigned groan instead. "Ugh. Alright. Fine! I'm not saying I approve of it but—" I pointed a finger right at her nose. "This is the absolute last time, okay?"

"Oh, thank you, thank you!" She threw her arms around me. "Thank you!"

***

It was hard for me not to feel guilty on any regular day. But it was harder today.

I was already smacking my hand against my forehead as I clattered down the dorm steps the next morning after being told that Lachlan had just arrived.

I was about to go and tell him that unfortunately, Wanda had some last-minute unavoidable plans and wouldn't be able to see him today again—like in the vaguest possible way.

I chewed on my bottom lip in anxiety. I was a bad actress and an even worse liar. But with any luck, Lachlan would just leave and I would finally be off the hook.

Please. Please. Please.

Arriving downstairs, I spotted a handful of girls at the lobby, by the way including Becca, our twenty-seven-year-old house chaperon and receptionist, all gathered around Lachlan.

Each one of them was smiling and laughing. *Flirting...?* I tilted my head, puzzled at the scene.

Lachlan had an enigmatic smile on his face, his hands casually shoved in his pockets, looking entirely attentive to whatever this girl Bridget Sanderson was talking about.

I gave him a once-over, for a moment trying to imagine what those other girls were seeing.

Lachlan's dark hair just barely fell across his forehead. His broad shoulders looked especially good in that long fleece overcoat. And somehow there was a hint of intensity in those puppy dog gray eyes Wanda had always singled out.

I wrinkled my nose, now baffled by Wanda's conundrum. She thought *this* guy was 'blah'?

When someone's story was punctuated by an eruption of giggles, I decided to approach the group, already tentative.

"Lachlan?"

He spun around. "Ashleigh." He looked surprised, glancing up the stairs as if to double-check that I was alone. "What are you doing here? Where's Wanda?"

"Um." I fidgeted in my stance, watching the congregation of girls gradually disperse around us. "Wanda had to go do this thing. It was a super last-minute emergency. I'm so sorry. She won't be able to meet with you today."

I was dreading seeing the disappointment on Lachlan's face again, also I was kicking myself at how bad my made-up excuse was. But this time, he just shook his head, almost knowingly. "She's avoiding me, isn't she?"

"No!" I frowned. "I mean, I'm sure she's excited to see you. It's been so long."

"Yes, it has." He took a deep breath, reaching up to rub the back of his neck as if in strain. "That's the problem, isn't it? She's probably forgotten all about me."

I pursed my lips. "Don't be too hard on yourself," I urged. "Long-distance relationships are always tricky."

"Yes, but it's my fault. I was the one who insisted on it. I was just so crazy about her." His gaze dropped to his shoes. "I should have known Wanda wasn't the type of person who could be tied down to a ghost."

He blew out a breath. "I bet she wasn't even happy to hear that I was visiting. I suppose that's my fault too. Not keeping in touch for so long. She must be feeling pretty angry with me."

Of course, I couldn't tell him exactly what Wanda's feelings actually were. "Well, I can't really say."

Lachlan glanced sideways up at me with a small smirk. "You don't have to say anything. It's all over your face."

My stomach felt queasy. "I'm so sorry."

He raked his fingers through his hair in quiet frustration. "So what, does she want to break up? Is she seeing other people?"

"No!" I shook my head. "I mean she definitely doesn't want to break up." I bit my lip. She's just happily entertaining stupid thoughts about that that someone may have thoughtlessly put in her head.

I grimaced. "You know that's really something you should talk to her about. She's just—maybe just give her some more time?"

"Time," he scoffed in mocking.

He looked so disillusioned and incredulous, I felt worse. "Look, I'm sure this is all just a misunderstanding and you two will be able to work it out."

Lachlan shot me an amused look. He could probably see right through my empty reassurances. But he just sighed in resignation. "If you say so."

He cast an absent glance around the lobby. "Well, I guess there's not much point waiting here." He jerked his thumb backward. "Do you want to go get something to eat?"

"What?"

"I'm starving." Lachlan motioned. "I saw this really interesting place just past campus."

I hesitated. I was already buried under my lame mountain of lies. If I had to stall any longer trying to suppress the truth about Wanda, I would likely implode.

He put up his hands. "Look, I promise I won't ask any more tough questions. And I'm sure Wanda owes you something. I'd be happy to pay it."

"Um..."

"Do you like brunch?"

My eyes must have lit up at the word, Lachlan had to chuckle.

"Looks like a yes."

5

Crepes

There was definitely something strange going on.

I couldn't help but think as I watched Lachlan, for the lack of a better term, flirt with the curly-haired waitress at the counter who seemed about our age.

I narrowed my eyes as he came back to our table beside the window that was decorated with fake snow.

"Sweet." Lachlan slid into the seat across from me. "Check out these chocolate straws Eileen added to my Yule log." He gestured to his Christmas-themed drink that was overflowing with jellybeans.

Sure. Out of the kindness of her own heart, I had to muse to myself.

But I didn't say anything as I simply stirred my coffee, and the moment Lachlan put down his drink, I automatically reached out to pluck a couple of marshmallows off it.

He stopped short, an amused look on his face, but he didn't say anything.

It took another two seconds for me to realize what I'd done. "Oh shoot! I'm so sorry. Force of habit." I considered putting the marshmallows back but then cringed instead as that would be obviously ridiculous.

Lachlan let out a chuckle. "Don't worry about it. Take some more if you like. I can always get extras."

Self-conscious, I clasped my hands together, only looking up again when a waiter came with trays of our food and he plunked the plates onto the table.

Lachlan was sipping on his straw. "Mm, I love the way they make these drinks. It's so fascinating to observe substances with different specific gravities interact within a glass container," he remarked.

Oh-kay, I couldn't help but knock his comment as I unwrapped my cutlery from the napkin, but then I stopped to stare at my plate.

Mushrooms, toast, spinach, scrambled eggs...

"Oh."

Lachlan, noticing my pause, looked up. "What?"

They had forgotten my side of bacon. I made a face in slight annoyance. I really had to stop adding sides to my meal as it was always the easiest way to screw up an order.

I blinked at the food. "Um, nothing."

"Nothing?" he repeated.

I dismissed, "No. It's fine."

"Fine? Then definitely something's wrong," he inferred.

I made another face, waving the topic away. "It's fine, really. They didn't give me my side order of bacon."

"Oh okay, so ask him to go check. Maybe they just forgot." He turned back to his own food, obviously under the impression that it was a simple thing that I could just do.

"Oh, I can't do that."

"Of course you can."

"Of course I can't." My pulse was already beginning to race in anxiety at the mere thought of having to explain the situation to someone. "Forget it. I can live without the bacon. I don't need the bacon."

"What?" He gave me a puzzled look but his gaze distracted away when the waiter came back to offer some fresh cracked pepper.

"Hey," Lachlan called out before the guy could walk away. "I'm so sorry to bother you but my friend's order seems to be missing a side order of bacon?"

With no fuss whatsoever, the waiter picked up my plate, saying, "Oh, sure, let me go see what happened."

And I watched the waiter disappear back through the kitchen, my shoulders slumping in relief.

Lachlan tilted his head to give me an amused look. "You can live without the bacon?" he repeated before narrowing his eyes. "Have you never sent back food at a restaurant before?"

My heart was literally still pounding in my chest. "No."

"Why not?"

I shrugged, at a loss. "Well, because..." I trailed off, unable to give an exact reason without sounding like a mental case.

Lachlan gave me a somewhat reassuring look even as he sliced into his meal. "It's really not a big deal, you know. I've waited at several restaurants before. Just don't be all rude about it."

"I'm never rude to the wait staff," I told him. That was, I never *spoke* to the wait staff. Ergo, never rude.

I shook my head briskly in an attempt to settle down, glancing over at the contents of Lachlan's plate. "Is that a pancake?"

"Nope, it's a breakfast crepe." He rubbed his hands together. "Honestly, I've been searching for this specialty crepe for months. I was sure I'd had it once before but I can't seem to remember where."

"Whoa, must be a pretty special crepe," I had to remark at his quest.

He shot me a *heck-yeah* look. "Absolutely! I've been ordering crepes everywhere all year to see if I can find it again but I've basically already ruled out every diner and café in Southern California."

"Oh, I thought you went to school in Florida?"

"No. I go to USC."

"Really? What do you study?"

"Engineering—robotics, A.I., that sort of thing."

I couldn't help my gawk. "Really?"

Wanda had said that Lachlan was smart but somehow I wasn't expecting this level of intellect for someone who was dating Wanda Meyers.

Lachlan was watching me. "Now you're trying to figure out how the heck Wanda and I started going out."

I met his gaze and let out a nervous chuckle. "I'm so sorry. Yes."

"Well, she must have told you about Camp Morningwater."

"Um, yes." I bit my lip, trying not to recall the detail within which Wanda had recounted some of those nights. "You guys were co-counselors together."

"It wasn't just that," Lachlan admitted. "Wanda helped me come out of my shell. I mean come on, I was a total nerd. I didn't have many friends—rather, I had *no* friends. I was invisible." He raked his fingers through his hair. "She was just so encouraging and cheerful and full of energy. I think she must have felt I needed rescuing."

The story struck a familiar chord with me. An invisible nerd who needed to come out of her shell? Maybe we could form a club.

"I just couldn't help but be drawn to her, you know? Wanda changed everything. She was always telling me to be more confident, more aggressive, more—"

"More self-assured?" I supplied as it was exactly what Wanda would keep saying to me as well.

He pursed his lips. "How do you know that?"

I had to shake my head in ridicule. "She says the exact same things to me all the time. She must think we're lost souls needing to be saved."

"Some of us are," Lachlan admitted with a chuckle. "If it wasn't for Wanda, I never would have had the courage to—" He stopped and instead waved it away. "Anyway, I just owe her a lot."

It was an effort to keep my jaw from dropping repeatedly in amazement.

Wow. Now I understood. This guy was so totes in love with Wanda.

A streak of guilt slashed my chest at the recall of exactly

where Miss Wanda was spending her free time lately and with whom.

I registered the wistful expression on his face, and aware that I might be opening that can of worms, I started anyway, "I'm so sorry about Wanda."

His forehead creased, likely with the weight of the grief that I already knew my statement would cause, and possibly even a silent confirmation of all his suspicions. He gave me a long look before responding softly, "It's not your fault."

I met his gaze. His eyes almost looked silver in the bright glare of the snow.

Fortunately, the waiter came back just then with my plate of food. "Here you go," he said. "We've also reheated the plate for you. Sorry for the inconvenience."

I stared at my food back on the table in front of me, breaking a pleased smile. I couldn't quite meet the waiter's gaze but I managed to mumble, "Thank you so much."

Lachlan didn't say anything but he had a smile on his face too as he went back to eating his food.

And for the third time, I seriously had to wonder what in the whole wide world could Wanda's problem possibly be with her super perfect boyfriend?

6

Gilbert

Near the end of the meal, that waitress came again with the bill and more extra freebies that Lachlan had 'scored.'

"Thanks, Eileen." Lachlan flashed a charming smile. "You're the best."

And there it was again.

I wrinkled my nose in suspicion. As soon as Eileen walked away, I gave Lachlan a look. "You're being really friendly to that waitress," I noted. "Do you know her?"

Lachlan's face blanked for a second before recovering. "Oh, sorry, no, it's just something I've observed. Flirting apparently gets you the best service."

I was taken aback by his confident response even as I pulled out some bills to pay for my half.

Lachlan was obviously a very smart guy. But that move felt to me like he was that average person who had recently discovered his superpowers but then decided to use them for evil.

"So what about you? What do *you* study?" Lachlan went on to prompt as though absolutely nothing was wrong.

"I..." I trailed off, my gaze distracting when the waitress came by again.

"Would your girlfriend like a free coffee refill?" Eileen asked with a sweet smile.

Note: At Lachlan. Not me.

She wasn't even actually interested to see if I wanted any more coffee.

But Lachlan returned the smile as he replied, "She's just a friend."

And Eileen's pearly white smile widened with eager delight. "Well, in that case," she began, her one hand retrieving her pen from her apron pocket, her other hand taking his before casually scribbling her number on his palm.

"Call me," she urged.

Lachlan didn't even look the least bit surprised.

But I sure as heck was.

I watched the entire exchange, my jaw having dropped the moment she'd pulled out that pen with the fluffy pink heart on one end.

And as soon as Eileen was gone, I shot Lachlan an incredulous look. "What the heck was that?"

"What?" Lachlan didn't seem to get it.

"What are you doing? Was that why you were flirting with that waitress? To get her number?" I accused.

"Hey, I didn't ask for her number. She just volunteered to give it to me."

"Well, sure, because you were totally leading her on," I remarked with a little scoff. "I can't believe this." I averted my gaze, feeling my faith in humanity slip a few points.

"It's alright," Lachlan reassured. "I've observed that a very little percentage of guys actually follow through with this sort of thing."

"What?" I blinked hard.

Jeez, this guy was seriously way too clever for his own good. He made it sound like what he had just done was completely rational and justified.

No wonder he and Wanda made such a great couple.

My jaw had dropped even lower but then I decided I didn't want to argue with his twisted logic.

I merely shook my head. "Never mind."

Lachlan furrowed his eyebrows, only seeming half-offended, maybe half-curious. "No, let's not never mind it. What did you want to say?"

I pursed my lips and gave him a pointed glare. "Does Wanda know you flirt with every girl you see?"

He *had* been doing it all day—at the boarding house too this morning and probably the other night with Becca as well.

But he lifted his shoulders. "It's no big deal. Who am I really hurting?"

I scoffed again in complete disbelief. "Your conscience? The truth?"

"But I wasn't lying."

"You're *omitting* the truth," I noted. "You know what, I think I'd better go now." I stood up, grabbing my jacket to put it on as I walked to the door.

"Hey!" He jumped up, nearly forgetting to put some more money on the bill tray before following me out the door.

"Ashleigh!" he called out. "I don't understand what just happened. Was there something wrong with being friendly?"

"Oh no, those little tricks don't work on me so don't even try," I warned. "You can't just charm your way out of everything."

That seemed to irk him. "Why not? Everyone else does it. Besides, I've seen complete assholes get away with more."

I spun around for a moment. "Oh, is that your goal?"

"Fine, I'm sorry. I never mean anything more by it. It's completely harmless!"

"Sure, but have some integrity." I seethed, glancing back at him, tugging my jacket closed over my neck.

Lachlan was purposefully keeping a few steps behind me, his hands shoved in his coat pockets, looking lost and dejected, those puppy dog eyes downcast all over again.

I blew out a breath in annoyance—and then guilt, of course.

Alright, fine. It wasn't like he did something terribly bad. I supposed a little harmless flirting never hurt anyone.

And he was probably right. That girl Eileen wouldn't even know any better. Lots of guys out there definitely get away with worse.

I didn't even know why I was so upset about it, why I felt so disappointed.

Maybe because Lachlan had surprised me.

Maybe because I had made a mistake, pigeonholing him into this perfect boyfriend of Wanda's, not accounting for maybe he was just a regular human guy.

It's not like he even—

"Oh, shoot." I ducked down, spotting a familiar face up ahead.

Gilbert Lawson was at the pedestrian crossing. Although, thank goodness, he hadn't seen me yet.

But Lachlan's eyes narrowed at me. "What is it?"

I clenched my teeth, despite cursing in my head. "Oh, nothing, it's just this guy. No big deal. He just kind of won't leave me alone."

I stepped back, trying to hunch behind Lachlan's tall form as we walked.

But when I peered around to see if the coast was clear, I accidentally met Gilbert's gaze and his eyes lit up, his gait instantly diverting toward us.

"Ashleigh!"

"Oh crap," I mumbled under my breath, straightened back up, trying to rack my brain for some way to escape but it was too late.

Gilbert was breathless, little white clouds puffing out of his mouth as he jogged over, already grinning. "Hi. I thought that was you. Weren't you going home for the holidays?"

He cast Lachlan a glance before his gaze settled on me again. "If I had known you'd be around, I would have invited you to our club's Quiz Night party."

My throat was dry. "Um…"

Lachlan slid his arm around my shoulders, his tone undisturbed. "Ash, I think you forgot to introduce me."

I snapped my attention up at him. "What? Oh. Um, Gilbert…this is…Lachlan." I met Gilbert's gaze again just as Lachlan decided to add something.

"I'm Ashleigh's boyfriend."

Stunned, I stilled under his grasp but Lachlan's expression remained as cool as the frost around us.

Gilbert's mouth dropped open so wide I could almost see his tonsils. "Oh." He blinked at me. "Oh."

I bit my lip, managing a nervous chuckle, but I didn't trust myself to say anything else.

I was in enough trouble spouting lies about Wanda nearly all morning. I wasn't going to volunteer any more lies about myself too.

But after a moment, Gilbert composed himself, narrowing his eyes at Lachlan. "No, you're not."

And my eyes widened, almost already in panic.

How could he possibly know either way?

Lachlan's eyebrows shot up. "I'm not?"

Gilbert sort of sneered at us. "No. Ashleigh likes blondes."

My own jaw dropped in incredulity. What the actual—?

And Lachlan turned amused eyes at me. "Oh, does she?"

I was barely able to stifle my chuckle, now in serious disbelief.

But Lachlan tugged me closer to him—close enough I could feel how warm he was, close enough he felt so solid against me.

"Well," Lachlan relayed. "I don't know where you get your information, Gilbert, but you should know, Ashleigh has made this one exception just for me."

Gilbert met my gaze again and I bit my lip again, trying to keep my composure. Gilbert's face looked like he had seen a ghost, like he couldn't believe his own two eyes.

Lachlan simply grinned, his eyes still pinned on Gilbert. "Bye, Gilbert."

Gilbert blinked again as though snapping out of a trance before he gave me a nod. "Uh-huh. See ya, Ash."

As soon as Gilbert had walked further enough to be out of earshot, I burst out laughing, looking up at Lachlan sideways in mirth and he started laughing too.

"Well. That should be that." He withdrew his arm from my shoulders.

"I can't believe you just did that. You are crazy."

Lachlan spoke up, indignant, "Oh, *I'm* the crazy one? What about stalker boy over there?"

"He's not a—" I stopped short, making a face. "Well, I guess I really didn't want to call him that but yeah...jeez."

It had never occurred to me to use that label but I supposed there were limits as to how much information people should have on other people.

"Seriously, what is the deal with that guy?" Lachlan jerked his thumb backward in the direction of the crossing we'd just passed. "And why didn't you just tell him you're not interested?"

"What?" I tried to wheedle. "I mean, he didn't technically ask me out. He's really not interested in me that way."

"Could have fooled me."

"Besides, I have a boyfriend," I relayed offhand.

"Oh, are we still playing that?"

I met his mischievous gaze. "Not you, crazy." I gave him a playful shove. "His name is Jason. He's from back home."

His eyebrows shot up. "Ah, I see. The blonde, I presume," he quipped with a mischievous smirk.

"Yes." I met his amused gaze. "Honestly, I have no idea how Gilbert could have even known about him. Jason's never been to visit me."

"Never?"

I shook my head, grateful that at least Lachlan had been around to proxy as my bodyguard in the absence of Wanda. "I'm so sorry you had to be involved in that. But you were brilliant," I had to remark in approval.

"My pleasure."

The tension in my shoulders dissipated as the two of us fell back into step to continue walking down the path together.

Lachlan was looking off to one side. There was a long pause before he spoke.

"Listen...I want to apologize if I did something inappropriate back at the diner." He let out a sigh. "A lot of this stuff is new to me, you know?"

"You know what?" I resolved with a careless shrug. "It was really none of my business." I put my hands up in defeat. "And now I owe you one so..."

His mouth curved into a diffident smile and I thought I caught a glimpse of that guy he used to be.

Strangely, what popped into my head was the marvel at how much impact knowing Wanda had had on him and wondering if this was my future too...

We had reached the corner when he spoke again. "Hey, isn't that the same guy from before?" Lachlan was trying not to make an obvious gesture toward the guy standing beside a light post who was trying in vain to be discreet.

I groaned in distaste. "Oh my gosh, is he following us?"

Lachlan glanced over his shoulder. "Oh yeah, he most definitely is."

My heart began to pound in anxiety again at the notion of another confrontation, and my friends' words at the diner came back to me as if of an epiphany.

Jeez, they must all be right. I really *wanted* to be nice to everyone. Even stalkers who were actually, legitimately in the wrong. I just wanted to walk on by, pretend he wasn't there, and deal with it another day.

Or maybe have Wanda deal with it another day.

But Lachlan had a different notion.

"I think maybe we should put him in his place."

"How?" I made a face, already uncomfortable about the idea. "I have no idea what to do."

"Maybe I do." Lachlan reached over to take my hand.

I bit my lip to laugh but didn't pull away. "What are you doing?" I hissed.

He grinned, not wanting to look right at Gilbert. "Is it working?"

I pretended to stretch my neck and spotted Gilbert again, shocked, dazed, and shaking his head.

The guy stood stock still, still puffing slightly in disbelief for a few moments before he finally turned and walked away.

I blew out a breath in relief. "He's leaving."

Lachlan let out a deep, throaty laugh. "I do admire his perseverance."

"Man, that is one tough customer." I shook my head again. "He's actually a nice guy. He's just...a little too intense."

Lachlan blew out a breath. "Wow, you're defending him. Alright."

I cringed again. Jeez. Was I?

My hand felt cold when he pulled his away, and when we crossed the next street, Lachlan put his hand on the small of my back to lead.

I figured he must have done it before. Except for this time, I was acutely aware of his touch.

I walked faster but he matched my pace and when a breeze blew past, I caught his scent—freshly-showered and all minty from that Christmas drink—and I couldn't help an involuntary shiver.

Uh-oh.

Then a heavy warm coat settled on my shoulders. "Hey—"

"You looked cold."

I blinked at him, surprised. "Oh. Thanks."

Goodness. This guy was chivalrous too?

I sneaked a sideways glance at him but he met my gaze and smiled.

Another shiver ran up my spine and I looked away.

Uh-oh.

We arrived at the front steps of our dorm building and I paused to shrug off his coat to give it back.

"Well, um, that was fun." Lachlan slid his coat back on, shoving his hands in the pockets again. "Thanks uh...for keeping me company."

"And thanks for helping me out with...you know." I curled my lips in distaste.

His smile widened in mirth. "My pleasure," he said again, his voice lowered.

My pulse was racing again. I couldn't help it. The

combination of those puppy dog eyes and that deep, rich voice was a killer.

Uh-oh.

7

One Dog

I stopped in the doorway of our room. It was still a horrendous mess, especially Wanda's side that I wouldn't have been surprised if there was a family of mice already living under the piles of laundry.

But my stomach was churning at what Becca from downstairs had just told me.

Apparently, I had missed a call from Jason.

Because I was out all morning with Lachlan.

Wanda's boyfriend.

I buried my face in my hands. What the heck was I doing?

I was getting a crush on my roommate's boyfriend.

I flopped facedown onto my bed with a groan, pushing aside near-empty packets of potato chips with a loud crinkle.

It was rationalizing time.

Of course, I would get a crush on Lachlan. Given this

morning's commotion, every other girl in our building probably already had a crush on him too.

He was sweet. He was cute. He was crazy smart. He had
the most adorable smile ever.

I shook my head briskly to clear it, checking back in
with reality.

It was fine. Everything was fine. Everything was alright.
This was completely normal.

Besides, nothing happened. Nothing was *going* to happen.

Also given what Wanda was probably doing with Doug,
it wasn't even entirely clear whether Wanda would care at
all anyway.

Still... I guessed I could understand where Wanda was
coming from.

She had barely seen or heard from her boyfriend for so
long, and sometimes when you don't see someone, maybe you
forget what they're like.

The last time I had spent any kind of time with Jason was
over six years ago, that summer after they had just moved.

We had taken a picnic to the beach. We'd talked and
laughed as though he wasn't even leaving, as though nothing
was going to change.

Even though Jason and I still kept in touch as often as
possible, every visit since then had been successively shorter
and more casual, the conversations more monotonous and
repetitive.

Was it also a mistake to assume everything would be
exactly the same as it was with us? Maybe I was putting too
many assumptions into our relationship as well.

To tell the truth, Jason hadn't even mentioned anything

about getting back together. All we had discussed so far was that we were going to see each other again.

As friends.

And maybe that's all he wanted to be.

I frowned against my sheets before pushing up on my elbows in exasperation, casting a dull glare around the room.

This mess totally needed to be cleaned.

I kicked at my sheets, coming up for air from the book I was heavily involved in and checked the digital clock.

4:30.

Absently, I reached out for a slice of pizza from the half-empty box beside me, watching the dark clouds loom in the sky out the window.

This was turning out to be a super bummer Christmas.

Oh, there she goes. I sat up in bed as I glimpsed Wanda walking up the front walk outside.

The girl who said this vacation stuck at school was supposed to be fun.

I spotted Doug jogging to catch up to her and when he leaned over to kiss her, I looked away, almost gagging on my pizza.

After a few minutes, Wanda breezed into the room, her gaze and mind completely adrift.

I gave her a few seconds to acclimate before raising my eyebrows in a prompt. "Nice day?"

Wanda looked over, surveyed the scene, noting the pizza box, the book, and me still in bed. "De Luca, what are you doing? This is what you do on a lovely evening like this?"

"Oh well, I'm sorry," I replied with all the sarcasm required. "I was supposed to be hanging out with my friend but she just totally abandoned me! Maybe you know her. Her name is Wanda Meyers."

Wanda let out an amused laugh, light as air. "You know you hide it well, but you can be so dramatic sometimes."

I rolled my eyes. "So how was the date?"

Her eyes lit up in an instant. "Oh, it was so romantic." She sank onto my bed. "For a big guy, I never thought Doug would be so graceful on the ice. I'm almost sorry I'm not a bad skater. It would have been just like one of those romance movies, you know?"

"Oh, yeah?" I feigned cooing before my face fell again. "What about Lachlan?" I asked in a stage whisper.

Wanda's face soured like I had thrown cold water all over her daydream and she let out a moan, collapsing onto my bed and exaggerating punching the mattress in agony a couple of times.

"Wanda!" I exclaimed. "You're going to have to face him sooner or later."

She sighed, straightening up and walking over to her bureau to get changed, ignoring me.

"Wanda," I repeated.

"Ugh, why do you have to be such a nag anyway?" Wanda complained.

My eyes widened. "Why?" I jumped up from bed to level my gaze with hers. "Because I'm the one who had to cover for you today. Again!" I threw up my hands. "Lachlan's not stupid. He can take a hint."

Wanda pursed her lips. "So what did you tell him?"

"I didn't tell him anything. *You* need to talk to him."

Wanda wailed, walking up to stand by the bathroom doorway. "Look Ash, I said I'll do it, I'll do it. I just have to find the right timing."

I studied her expression. "So *are* you going to break up with him?" I asked, keeping my tone as neutral as humanly possible.

She took a long deep breath. "Well."

"Well?" I prompted, switching gears. "Let's make this simpler. Do you like Doug more than Lachlan now?"

Wanda's face scrunched up for a few moments and her response was lackluster. "Meh."

I blinked. "Meh? What does that mean?"

She shrugged, blowing out another breath. "Well, I don't know! Doug is just not..." she trailed off, wrinkling her nose.

I rolled my eyes in disbelief. "Two dates and you're already bored with him? Jeez, Wanda!"

"I mean Doug can be such an oaf sometimes. He is so not a gentleman."

Oh great, was it time to compare the two guys? One guess as to who won that round.

My stomach even clenched at the recall of Lachlan giving me his coat this afternoon when I hadn't even asked.

"And he's not exactly the smartest tool in the shed," she went on.

I pursed my lips, bobbing my head in agreement.

More points to Lachlan.

"But I knew that already," she dismissed with a wave of her hand.

"So...?" I gestured for her to go on.

"But Locky's just so..." Wanda trailed off again, her fore-head wrinkling as she tilted her head in deep thought.

I must have been glaring at her for a while that she winced when she met my gaze again and put her hands up in defeat. "Alright, alright, fine!" she resigned. "I'll talk to Locky tomorrow. I assume he's dropping by again?"

"He didn't say."

"Is he still as cute as ever?" Wanda asked, her gaze turning dreamy all over again.

I had to wince myself. "Cuter." I had to bite my lip, resist-ing the powerful urge to elaborate.

Wanda let out a dramatic half-groan, half-sigh. "Wanda, Wanda, Wanda." She shook her head as she plucked the piece of paper with Lachlan's number on it off the bureau, walking over to the phone. "So many men, so little time."

8

Another Last Favor

There were times when I really wished I was invisible.

On a regular school day, the sunroom at the boarding house was a nice, quiet place to read a book, or do some last-minute work on a school paper alongside your peers, or have group meetings to organize the next hot button issue protest rally.

But today, with most of the students away and fewer busybodies around, Yvette had decided to cancel the "nice and quiet" part of that description.

I moved seats for the fifth time since everywhere I'd sat down since I cracked open my book was apparently exactly where Yvette wanted to sit as well.

It didn't make any sense since there was literally nobody else in the room except the two of us.

I knew she was just doing it to mess with me and I wasn't responding or letting her get to me because I figured she would eventually get bored and give up, except it wasn't happening yet.

Yvette sidled up to my chair at the long study table again. "Oh, that's my seat."

I managed not to roll my eyes. Jeez. Did she have absolutely nothing else to do today?

I cleared my throat, not meeting her gaze, and stood up, this time walking over the side of the room to stand and read by the spotlight lamp.

Only to have Yvette walk over and hover closely over my book, overwhelming me with the scent of her caked-on eye make-up. "So?" she prompted with a smug sneer after a few seconds. "How do you like The Alchemist?"

I gave her a wary look, not under any illusion she was actually interested, but replying nonetheless. "Um, it's really good."

Yvette let out a snarky chuckle but before she could say anything more Wanda burst into the room as if in shock.

"Yvette! What are you doing out? The sun is up!"

I was caught so off-guard by the joke that I almost choked on my laughter.

Yvette shot each of us a mocking smirk before slinking back out the door.

Wanda's eyes narrowed, watching Yvette leave before turning her pointed glared toward me.

"What?" I asked innocently.

"You know, at some point, you're going to have to tell that girl to go stuff herself."

I put my hands up. "She was just being annoying. No big deal."

"Sure. Keep telling yourself that." Wanda rolled her eyes. "I just wish I could be around when you finally explode."

"Look, acknowledging her is just reinforcing her negative attention-seeking behavior," I rationalized.

"Whatever." She waved her hand before moving to twirl around, gesturing to her argyle cardigan and white pleated skirt, screaming college preppy. "But seriously, how do I look?"

I tilted my head with an amused smile at her seeming attempt to "match" nerdy Lachlan. "You look great. When do you ever not?"

She bit her lip, sort of fidgeting in her stance and I narrowed my eyes at her in curiosity.

"Are you nervous?" I had to ask.

Wanda gave me a telltale look I had only ever seen on very rare occasions.

"I honestly can't understand you," I remarked. "First, you act like you don't even want to see your boyfriend, and now this?"

"Well, I still want to make a good impression," Wanda supplied. "I mean, we've got so much to catch up on, don't you think?" she added with a wink.

Ugh.

Although despite all that, I couldn't help a chuckle under my breath.

This morning, I had woken up with my mind perfectly crystal clear.

Crushes, much like flirting, could be totally harmless. And, much like Wanda, I was probably just missing "that magic."

I had managed to get Jason on the phone for a while

this morning. He was rushing off to help his mom do some last-minute shopping but just hearing his familiar, reassuring voice already filled all the wanting nostalgic voids inside me. And I was back to looking forward to seeing him again at New Year's.

Until then, all I needed was enough of a useful preoccupation and to not get pulled into anybody else's drama.

"Look," Wanda began, peering at her own reflection in one of the knick-knack cabinets. "I'm sorry about checking out on you so much this week. I know I promised you a great vacation and instead, I've been mostly—distracted."

"Uh-huh."

She turned to grasp my hands. "But I will totally make this up to you. I promise." She winked again.

"Don't worry about it," I dismissed. "My flight finally got confirmed for Sunday, just enough time for me to make it to New Year's Eve so you won't have to shirk on babysitting me for much longer."

"Don't be silly. Let me just catch up with Locky first and then the three of us can go do something—maybe take a bus down North End way. I know you love it there."

My eyes widened a slight. "Oh, I said don't worry about it. Besides, I'm going over to Stella's today to help set up for her parents' Boxing Day gala."

"What? Is that tonight?"

"Well, I didn't know what you had planned this week."

"Well, I didn't know I would have all this going on." She gestured absently around the sunroom. "I mean the last time Locky came for a visit was like a year ago."

"I remember."

"Do you remember when we did that harbor cruise on one of those authentic big boats? Locky felt seasick but he was so embarrassed, he wouldn't tell anyone." Her mouth curved into a smile at the memory. "He's just always been so awkward and shy. It's so adorable."

"Mm-hm." I nodded, not bringing up that I had been just as green around the gills the first time Wanda had dragged me onto that same cruise. "He actually told me you helped him come out of his shell. He sounded really grateful."

"Oh, isn't he just the sweetest?" Wanda cooed, her hands on her cheeks.

"Yes." I sighed, not even attempting to reconcile her gushy comments with the fact that she had ditched the same guy to date someone else yesterday.

But I reminded myself to stay out of it. "Hey, listen, I'm really glad you decided to finally talk to Lachlan." I gave her a short pat on the back. "Let me know how it goes. I'll probably be at Stella's all day."

"Wanda Meyers!" Becca called out from the lobby and we both looked up.

"Must be Mr. Boyfriend there right now," I guessed, nodding toward the doorway.

"Ooh, fabulous." Wanda nodded, blowing out a breath as she turned to leave.

After a few moments, Wanda's laughter floated back toward the sunroom and I figured that things must be going well.

I was honestly glad she was going to put that poor guy out of his misery.

I packed up my stuff, walking over to grab my jacket off the rack in the corner, preparing to head off myself.

"Pst," I heard behind me and I spun around.

Wanda was peeking back into the room. "I need a huge favor."

"What?" I made a face. "Whatever happened to 'you'll never ask me for anything ever again'?" I peered over her shoulder to check out the guy standing at the counter.

I sucked my breath in. "That's Doug!"

"Duh, Ashleigh." Wanda rolled her eyes. "Look, I have to go. Doug has a surprise for me," she relayed, her eyes shining.

My eyes widened—in dismay, in trepidation. "What? What about Lachlan? Wanda, you said—"

"Look, Ash, I really gotta go," Wanda rushed on. "I'll deal with Locky later. Tell him—tell him something."

Ugh! I groaned out loud in exasperation but it was no use as Wanda and Doug's footsteps clunked down the lobby tiles and the front door swing shut.

I stood for a few moments, still holding all my stuff, dumbfounded, and some of Stella's choice words came back to me.

Don't let yourself get sucked into her demented world. You'll never escape.

This was just great.

Anything was better than this.

I recognized Lachlan's voice instantly as soon as he spoke to Becca and I spun back around, bracing myself against the sunroom door to hide.

Tell him 'something' had been Wanda's directive. I had to think of 'something.'

Or...I could just not, I considered after a moment. I could just wait for Lachlan to give up waiting and leave then I could sneak out the back somehow.

Wanda could deal with her own fallout. There was no reason for me to get even more involved in her drama.

Sound like a good plan? Perfect.

Except Yvette and two of her emo friends decided to walk into the sunroom just then. I noted Yvette's sweeping glance before her pleased smile.

Yep. Wanda was gone. I was alone.

I bit my lip in serious alarm, walking backward out of the sunroom—and bumping right into a tall, immovable wall.

Of Lachlan.

"Ashleigh?" He sounded surprised.

I froze, cringing for a moment, before putting on what I hoped was a calm and friendly expression for Lachlan's sake as I spun around. "Hey, you."

He broke a bright smile. "I'm supposed to be meeting Wanda. Is she upstairs?" He cast a glance up the way.

I wrinkled my nose again. "Uh...Wanda?" I feigned innocence. "She left early. Said she had something to do. I assumed she was already with you."

Lachlan's face clouded over, his smile disappearing.

I debated whether or not to sneak away right then and there. This was exactly the fallout that I wanted not to have to deal with.

But the look on his face was just so despondent. It was as though he was going through so many things in his head all at once. I was almost amazed steam wasn't coming out of his ears. He seemed to be calculating exactly what this latest brush-off could mean and probably figuring it all out.

I swallowed hard, peering at him. "Are you okay?"

"No."

I winced again. But I didn't leave.

He closed his eyes for a moment before going again. "No," he huffed. "How can she expect me to just—?" He groaned. "I am so done with this." He whirled around to leave.

I made another face. "Hey, she really did plan to see you today, I swear," I called out, relieved I was actually not lying to him for once.

Lachlan paused in mid-stride.

My heart pounded in my chest. Whatever the reason, I didn't want him to leave in an angry huff. "Would you give her one last chance?" I suggested, attempting to mirror the same pleading look that Wanda had employed with me. "Please?"

I wasn't ready for the full intensity of his gaze to land on me when it did.

He was upset. He was confused. He was trying really hard to tamp it down. I almost wanted to pat his arm in consolation, or you know, hug him.

But after a long moment, he dropped his gaze with a sigh.

"You're a really good friend."

Oh, I don't know about that.

That comment snapped me back to reality and I began to sidestep away. "Um, I'm so sorry but I have to go now. I have to be somewhere."

He followed me with his gaze, disoriented. "Oh?" His forehead creased. "Do you want some company?"

I stilled.

"Where are you going?"

"Um...I'm going to help out a friend to do preparations for a party. It's more like chores. It probably won't be fun." I waved it away.

"I don't mind." Lachlan grimaced. "My friend where I'm staying is sort of getting on my nerves." He rubbed the back of his neck in strain. "He's really into online gaming and if I have to hear him yell 'pwn some noobs' over and over again all day, I might actually set the house on fire."

"Oh."

What was the worst that could happen?

9

Party preps

This. This was the worst that could happen.

I was laughing as we crossed the Common.

Lachlan was trying, in earnest I thought, to enunciate in the local accent, putting all his r's in the wrong places but it was just making me crack up all over again.

Walking the one mile to Stella's house was almost unbearable—in that, I was pretty sure I could bear ten more miles just to keep walking with him.

I was having to spend every other minute consciously trying to maintain a list of his flaws as opposed to a list of everything we had in common—and there was *a lot*—all the while the darn cut of his jaw kept peeking out from above his scarf as he strode beside me.

"No, but I still wish someone had told me beforehand that we were going on a Freedom Trail walking tour, you know, instead of a zombie scavenger hunt."

I could barely talk, I was laughing so hard. "I know, right?"

"I was just glad nobody could recognize me under all that zombie makeup that I absolutely *had* to put on." He feigned a roll of his eyes.

I put my finger up, struggling to keep my laughter at bay. "That was a particularly amazing tour though. I just love that beautiful, old architecture."

"I know, right?" he beamed. "I mean the detail on some of these buildings." He paused to amend, "You know, what all I could see past my fake bloody eyeball—"

And I burst out laughing all over again. "You were a total champ."

He gave me a suffering look as if in offense before he started laughing too.

When we crossed the next street, he took my arm in his.

For safety. Probably.

My pulse raced anyway.

Whilst I still maintained that a majority of this was Wanda's fault, I couldn't help but want to kick myself.

What was I thinking letting him come to Stella's today? Nothing good was going to come out of this.

But it was too late now.

"This is where your friend lives?" Lachlan whistled, eyeing the navy blue, four-story apartment building with the white gothic revival curved sash windows right up ahead.

"Oh. Yeah." I stepped back to follow his impressed gaze. "Stella's parents own this Fortune 500 company and every year, around Boxing Day, they throw this charity fundraiser."

"Nice." He nodded as if in approval. "Looks like they could

afford to hire people to do all the setup. Why are you guys doing it?"

"Oh, they do have staff to do it too. We used to just hang out and help for fun. But now, Stella's studying Interior Design and she's just started a Party Planning business. Her parents thought this would be a great hands-on experience for her. Anyway, she loves to do it."

The two of us walked up the steps of the federal-style front porch and I pressed the doorbell, peering in through the fixed glass windows beside the door.

I spotted Stella's mom come down the foyer and when she swung the door open, an assault of powdery perfume wafted out.

"Ashleigh," she greeted with a melodious purr and a smile, the Swarovski crystal beads on several bracelets rattling on her wrist as she gestured Lachlan and me in through the doorway.

"Merry Christmas, Mrs. H," I beamed.

"Dear, it's so good to see you again." Mrs. Hoffman turned over her shoulder. "Stella! Your friends are here!"

Stella's footsteps clattered coming down a staircase. "Who is it?"

"It's Ashleigh, dear." Mrs. Hoffman's eyes crinkled as her smile widened at me before turning to Lachlan. "And this must be—"

"Lachlan," Lachlan supplied, putting his hand out to shake.

"That's right. You must be Ashleigh's boyfriend."

My eyes bulged and I met Lachlan's just as wide-eyed gaze. "Oh, actually—"

But before either of us could correct her, she yelled out again. "Magda, I'm going now!"

Stella had arrived in time to overhear her mom's incorrect guess and she gave Lachlan and me a surprised look. "What? This is your boyfriend?

Lachlan and I were both already shaking our heads but Mrs. Hoffman was forging on in a hurry. She leaned over to kiss Stella on the cheek. "Dad went to get the car. We'll be back later, Sweetie." She turned back to us. "Kids, thank you so much for helping Stella and Spencer out with this."

My manners kicked in and I responded with a grateful look. "Oh, thanks for having us over, Mrs. H. We'll try to leave your Cristal alone this time."

"What, dear?"

Stella's eyes widened in alarm and she nudged her mom's shoulder out the door. "I'll see you later, Mom," she bade, mocking a salute.

"Bye, darling." Mrs. Hoffman swept past us with a whirl-wind of rattling beads and perfume before disappearing through the door.

"Mom just leave?" Spencer asked as he and Pete came down the hallway on the right. "Hey, did I hear Jason is here?" he asked, noting the guy he didn't recognize standing beside me.

"That's not Jason," Pete pointed out.

Lachlan shook his head.

I rolled my eyes. "No."

"So Jason's not here?"

"No. That's Ashleigh's new boyfriend," Stella supplied.

"You have a new boyfriend? Since when?" Pete was scratching his head.

"No! Don't be ridiculous. He is *not* my new boyfriend—"

Lachlan blinked a wince as though in offense. "Uh—"

"What, is he an old boyfriend?" Stella prompted, wrinkling her nose and turning to Spencer. "Why would she bring an old boyfriend here?"

"Maybe they're getting back together," Spencer replied with a shrug.

"Hey!" I clapped my hands sharply. "Jeez, everyone's all confused. Guys—" I took a deep breath in incredulity, motioning *do-over* with my hands before gesturing to Lachlan again. "This—is Wanda's boyfriend."

I relayed the next bit with a hint of caution in my tone, "You know the one from Florida?" trying to tell Stella, Pete, and Spencer what I meant with my eyes.

Ixnay on the Ougday?

But Spencer's eyes nearly popped out of his head. "Wanda's what?" Then he got a hold of himself. "Oh, oh!" He did a double-take in understanding. "Right. Okay. Well, it's nice to finally meet you..."

"Lachlan," Lachlan supplied again with a nod.

I blew out a breath in exasperation before gesturing to my friends to complete the introductions. "That's Stella, Pete, and Spencer."

"Hey, Lachlan. It's good to meet you, man." Pete gave him a nod in acknowledgment.

"Right. Lachlan," Stella repeated with a smile. "Well, then now I'm really curious as to how Ashleigh lured you to come along today to help out with these chores?"

I grimaced, afraid my guilt showed on my face. Did she really have to use that word? "I didn't *lure* him—"

But Spencer shot me a knowing look, patting my arm, fully in jest. "Sure you didn't."

Pete and Stella laughed. They were obviously just trying to mess with me but my mind was already reeling with all sorts of excuses and explanations.

Lachlan was all cool about all the ribbing though and he flashed that smile again. "Actually, it was either this or a day of mostly violent yelling from my roommate. Ashleigh's really saving *me* today."

He said that while thumping twice on my back like I was his best bud in the whole entire world.

I gave myself a mental shake, willing all my anxiety to settle the heck down.

Stella laughed again. "Aha. Good choice. Well, come on in, guys."

We put our coats away and she led us all the way upstairs to the huge double-height main salon with the near-floor-to-ceiling windows, glossy wooden furniture, and sparkling teardrop chandeliers.

It was hard not to notice Lachlan's awed expression, his mouth having dropped open.

Though honestly, even after all this time, I still never quite stopped being impressed myself.

The festive salon was already glittering with classy gold and silver boughs, balls, and bows, and the big (albeit fake) white Christmas tree down the end whilst still bare was already stunning and twinkly.

Pete and Spencer strode across the room to coordinate

the several staff who were purposefully bustling up and down the salon.

Stella headed over to a setup of tables in one corner with a mess of machines and cables on and around it.

"You got here just in time, Ash," she began, tapping on a single laptop key repeatedly, loudly, in frustration. "I've been trying to get the sound system to work for the last half hour."

I walked over and she stepped aside so I could peer at the screen. "Looks like the computer fell off the wifi network." I narrowed my eyes, rhythmically tapping on the keyboard.

"Scan the network again."

I jumped slightly, not noticing that Lachlan had come up beside me to peer at the screen too. "Oh. Yeah." I glanced up sideways at him. "I just did that. I think it needed to be cycled."

"Dude, I don't even understand what language she's speaking right now," Stella drawled before turning a curious look at Lachlan. "How do *you* know all that stuff? What do you study?"

"Robotics engineering. Over at USC."

Stella had about the same expression on her face as I had when I found out.

"Wow. Really? That's...unexpected. How are you dating Wanda again?"

Lachlan's gaze flickered to me for a split second but he just shrugged, apparently unwilling to share any further details with any more strangers. "Just lucky, I guess?"

I resisted the urge to scoff. More like, Lachlan was probably sick of having the exact same conversations with people. Not that I could blame him.

Also, and to wit, it was likely not a great idea to open the floor up to questions with regards to the status of his and Wanda's decidedly ambiguous relationship at the moment.

"How's it going?" Lachlan leaned over, close enough that his face was level to mine.

I cleared my throat out loud, trying to drag my focus back onto what I was doing and I clicked on a few more things. "Someone's gone and messed up the firewall settings. It should be..." I trailed off, watching the spinning circle on the screen.

"There it is." I looked up in expectation as the sound system across the salon came to life with soft, jazzy Christmas music streaming out and I smiled, straightening up in self-satisfaction.

"Woo!" Stella came over to pile on me from behind in the guise of a hug. "You're amazing!"

"Aah!" I shrugged her off. "Get off!"

That made Lachlan laugh.

Stella brushed her hair out of her face as she hopped off, still with a big grin. "You know Ashleigh's always been the only tech-savvy one among us," she told Lachlan. "She's going to make me a killer backdrop video for the party and I get to take all the credit."

"It's not that hard, Stella. I'm sure you could do it," I stated.

"Nuh-uh. I tried last year—remember Spencer, how did that turn out?" she asked aloud, glancing up.

"Ug-ly!" he called out from across the salon.

I laughed in resignation. "Fine. I'll do it." I moved to prop myself upon the bar stool beside the table, already nudging the laptop closer to me.

"You know I love you, babe," she cheered with a wink. Then she gestured underneath the table. "Hey, Miss Incredible. Maybe you can fix that too."

I checked out the set of machines with all manner and colors of wires in a tangled spaghetti mess on the floor. "Whoa, that is way out of my league."

But Lachlan followed my gaze and gave a casual shrug, already rolling up his sleeves. "I could do it."

I shot him a surprised look. "No. Hey, you can just hang out if you want. I wasn't really planning to force you to help out."

He narrowed his gaze at me in feigned overconfidence. "Hey, you're not the only tech-savvy one in the group today, you know?"

My jaw dropped in mocking at the apparent thrown gauntlet. "Oh—oh you're going to show off now? Be my guest."

Lachlan merely grinned in response before prompting, "Stella, how can I help?"

Stella slid over with a gleam in her eyes, her hands clasped together. "Well, our tech guy Theo usually runs some kind of cloudy system for the charity donations drop box..." she trailed off, unsure about her terminology before dismissing it. "Anyway, it's got all messed up during transport. Unfortunately, Theo says he won't be back until seven-ish."

Lachlan gave the setup a critical once-over as if forming some plan of attack in his head first.

"I think he called it some kind of array or something," Stella added.

"A redundant array for the network-attached storage.

Looks like the drives need to be plugged into the bays and then hooked up to the Ethernet first."

I watched him crack his knuckles, unable to help the stir in my stomach. Somehow hearing him describe the NAS drive was incredibly hot.

"Yeah! Whatever. That." Stella waved her hand. "Alright then, Mr. Engineering, time to show us what they teach you all over at USC."

Lachlan noticed me staring and met my gaze with another smile. That snapped me back to attention and I honestly had to reluctantly drag my focus back to the laptop screen.

10

Impressive

Stella had stepped away to attend to something so I assumed Lachlan's question was directed at me.

"So," he started, crouching under the table in an attempt to untangle the spaghetti wires. "That was pretty good what you did to that laptop. Do you take Computer Sciences courses at school?"

I was half-worried he was going to electrocute himself under there but I dismissed my concerns before replying, "Oh. Well, I actually wanted to do that. But it would be a significant shift on my course load."

"So shift it."

I had to laugh. It never ceased to amaze me the relative ease with which other people could suggest completely changing lives that were entirely not their own.

"Sure, I'll get right on that."

Lachlan slid back out from under the table, already grinning in recognition of my wry tone. "What's the matter?"

I rubbed my forehead. "The matter? Nothing. It's just...my parents and I had always planned for me to go into medicine. Biochemistry research."

His eyes narrowed, repeating my words. "Your parents *and* you always planned? What about just you?" he prompted.

I shrugged, unwilling to get into this debate again as I'd already had it plenty with my friends for years.

"Computer Sciences is a pretty impressive course. Your parents might be okay with it. Have you even asked them yet?" he suggested.

Stella overheard the last bits of our conversation as she and Pete walked back to our end of the salon approaching my table. "No way! Ashleigh is way too polite to do that. Haven't you noticed?"

"She avoids confrontations like the plague," Pete chimed in.

Lachlan's forehead creased in amusement. "Oh, is that why she can't even talk to restaurant staff to return food when it's perfectly acceptable?"

Stella laughed, elbowing me. "Dude, this guy is so perceptive."

I had to roll my eyes. "Thanks a lot, friends. I really appreciate the personal attacks."

"Aww, we're just trying to look out for you, Ash," Stella cooed, putting her arm around my shoulder to shake me. "We want you to be happy."

"That's right," Lachlan agreed as he straightened up again to make his point. "Think about how much stress you're putting yourself under from holding things back."

"Exactly," Stella agreed with a nod.

"Take it from me," Lachlan proposed. "You'd just feel so relieved to be able to be yourself and not worry about so many things."

I put my hands up. "I'm not saying you're wrong. I'm just saying...it's hard."

"I say take the leap anyway," Pete piped up as he bent down to haul a packing box into his arms. "Anything's hard until you do it once."

"Hey, leave her alone," Stella chided, her tone still mischievous. "I'm sure Ashleigh will grow a backbone when she's good and ready."

Lachlan went on, "Sure. You just need someone willing to give you that encouragement and support—"

"Support, Pete, not pushing," I echoed, giving him a pointed look and meeting Stella's gaze, making her laugh.

"Hey, I'll support the heck out of you right now—"

"Just like I had from Wanda," Lachlan added.

I stiffened and as I'd expected, that comment brought the entire conversation to a screeching halt.

It took a few seconds of awkward silence before Stella's sense of being a good hostess kicked in.

"Oh hey," she piped up, her eyes wide. "Is anyone hungry? Pete, maybe you could go see if catering could get us some snacks."

Pete's eyes popped in understanding and he jumped to the task. "As you wish."

Nervous, I met Stella's wan smile before glancing over to check how much of that Lachlan had noticed but he had gone back to setting up the machines and all he asked was, "Ash, is the red light on the UPS on?"

I leaned over to one side to check for him. "Yes."

"Well." Lachlan straightened up, dusting off his hands. "That should work now." He flicked a switch and his eyes lit up in satisfaction as a constant hum emanated from the machines.

"Can you check if the network can detect the NAS drive now?" He moved to stand beside me to see for himself.

I nodded, checking the settings on the screen before breaking a grin. "Yup. They're on. You did it."

"Nice." Grinning back, he gave me a high-five. "Now Theo just needs to configure it when he arrives."

"Fantastic!" Stella whooped, clapping her hands in glee. "You guys are rock stars!"

She tilted her head to study the immaculate new setup of the servers and the color-coded wires, certainly a stark difference from its initial state. "Wow, I can't even believe someone our age could do all that. Lachlan, you are so amazing."

Stella's face looked so enraptured. I had to roll my eyes. "Alright, settle down."

She waved me away and turned to Pete who was on his way back with Spencer. "Hey Pete, guys," she called. "You'll never guess what Lachlan just did."

Lachlan's face slightly flushed red but I noted that he looked pleased.

I bit back a smile, going back to setting up the video presentation for Stella but I caught her pointed look at me behind Pete.

He's great! she mouthed with an approving wiggle of her eyebrows.

I stifled my chuckle. Like I didn't already know that.

Lachlan noticed the brief exchange and gave me a questioning look. "What?"

"Oh. Nothing." I dismissed, pretending to scratch my nose to hide my sticking my tongue out at Stella in response.

He *was* great. *Juuust great.*

I was trying to think of a different metaphor for how time flies when not only are you having fun, but you're also working with a hot, new crush.

One who just seemed to keep getting even hotter as the day wore on, whom with every smile, I almost completely forgot he was currently attached to my roommate.

Lachlan's deep chuckle floated from across the salon, drawing my gaze for like the millionth time and I shook my head yet again.

He was standing near the snack table, one hand in his pocket, talking to the blond caterer chick.

Lachlan had been helping her set up, you know because he's that helpful.

Of course, Ms. Caterer had other ideas to fill the time.

Stella glanced up and narrowing her eyes, she rolled her chair toward me. "Is that what I think it looks like?" she asked under her breath.

"Oh. Yeah. He does that," I replied. "He has this theory about how flirting gets you the best service. He seems to apply it more often to food servers." I paused to muse, "Which if you think about it is actually its most advantageous use."

"Hm," Stella harrumphed from beside me. "Earlier, he was advising Pete about the most optimal ways to stock boxes—something about balancing the center of gravity," she told me, her tone already bemused before she held up a finger, "*while* holding the door open for me because he says that even with the conversation around feminism, he's observed that many women still appreciate chivalry now and then."

"Yup. Sounds like Lachlan." I had to chuckle.

Stella simply shook her head to herself as she rolled back away in her chair toward the other end of the table to focus on some paperwork.

When I cast another absent glance over at the snack table though, I could tell by Lachlan's body language that he was now trying to extricate himself from the situation.

He gestured away a couple of times, teetering on his stance intending to step away, but she must have been regaling him with some unmissable catering banter that he kept stepping back.

I chewed on my bottom lip as I watched the scene. I really shouldn't, I thought. I *really* shouldn't.

But I pushed off my seat and strode over to them, compelling a semblance of confidence in my gait.

"Hey, babe." I slipped my arm through Lachlan's and felt him freeze up for a moment. "Did you help Spencer put all those empty boxes back into storage yet?"

I gave the blond a sweet smile at the same time that I reached over to pick a strawberry from a platter to pop into my mouth.

But Lachlan only looked dazed for a split second before replying, "Oh. Uh, not yet." He pulled his arm away from me and I started, half in a panic that he wasn't going to go along with my ruse. Then Lachlan slid his arm around my waist instead.

Trying to tamp down the shivers from his touch all over again, I gave the blond another smile, glancing down to check her nametag. "Thank you for doing such a great job, Chloe. Stella's just going through the final orders for tonight right now."

Chloe was looking back and forth between Lachlan and me, obviously displeased, but I supposed she wasn't ready to give up on him just yet. Her gaze settled on me. "Are you his...?"

I tilted my head before putting my hand out to shake hers. "I'm his girlfriend. Nice to meet you."

Lachlan's fist clenched at my waist. He cast Chloe a tight smile before directly veering me away. "Um, see you, Chloe. Thanks."

I was already giggling before we were even out of earshot and Lachlan gave me a stunned look.

I gave him a no-nonsense look. "And now we're even."

His shoulders shook in mirth and those clear gray eyes were on me again, studying my face in amazement and, I was guessing, probably relief.

But before he could say anything, I noticed Spencer waving from across the room and I pulled away with a start.

"Oh, Spencer really does need your help with those boxes," I told him with a small grimace.

"Oh. Right. Thanks." Lachlan blinked, nodding before he

turned to head over to the other end of the salon, his hands stuck back in his pockets.

I had just slid back onto the barstool to go back to finishing my work when Stella pushed up from her chair to sidle up against me, her voice lowering. "Heyyy, so..."

I could see the already mischievous glint in Stella's eyes. She had obviously seen the whole thing.

"So?" I raised my eyebrows in a prompt.

"So," she echoed in exasperated mocking. "So what the heck was that?"

I shrugged to dismiss it. "Nothing. I owed him one."

Her mouth dropped open. "Seriously? That's all I get?"

I pointed to the laptop. "Stella, I'm working now."

But she wouldn't let it go. She dug her elbow in my side. "Lachlan's pretty cute."

That woke up the butterflies in my stomach again but I kept my focus on the screen, managing to sound neutral in my response. "Yeah. Of course."

I mean, duh. He *was* Wanda's boyfriend.

She narrowed her eyes at me. "I mean he's kind of great."

I bobbed my head in passive agreement, not taking the bait.

"I mean he's too good for Wanda...?" Stella proposed with a sing-song tone.

I sighed, pausing. "Noted. Thanks."

"Ugh! Ash, I might just actually wring your neck." She threw up her hands. "Don't you think he should be with someone who's going to appreciate him?" she prompted. "You know, someone he has more in common with? Someone whose company he's also been clearly enjoying." She gave me a pointed look.

"Dude, don't be reading into any of that stuff. All that flirting is totally fake. I told you Lachlan's pretty analytical and he's really good at maneuvering through certain situations to get him the most benefit."

"Alright." Stella's eyes widened in slight annoyance at my sound logic. "Let's flip it around then, shall we?" She met my gaze evenly. "Clearly, Wanda is not satisfied with this poor, homely lad. And as Wanda's friend, wouldn't you want her to be with someone who actually ticks her boxes?"

I merely shook my head in incredulity. "I love how you think this decision is suddenly up to me."

Stella turned to brace her hands on my arms, her eyebrows already raised in a solemn prompt. "Ashleigh, it is up to you. We all know Wanda's sticking her tongue down some random jock's throat right now—"

"Sshhh!" I shushed her.

"She doesn't deserve him," Stella hissed.

"You're just saying that because you don't like Wanda," I reminded her. "And you haven't heard how she talks about him."

Stella crossed her arms over her chest. "Regardless," she insisted. "And maybe you don't see it but he's totally looking at you the same way too."

"The same way as what?"

"Come on, Ash. I'm pretty familiar with those side glances that you think are so discreet. I can tell you like him."

I fought down my blush, giving her a suffering look to try to disguise it but unable to defend myself properly.

Stella's hand went thump on my shoulder. "Look, I know we give you a lot of flack about being too nice. But it's only

because we know you deserve way more than you give yourself. And you can't always just wait for someone else to give
happiness *to* you. Sometimes you have to take it."

I fidgeted in my seat. It might have been good advice but
coming from her right then, it sounded conniving and sneaky.

"Let's flip it around again, shall we?" Stella proposed. "Put
yourself in Wanda's shoes. If the situation were reversed, you
already know exactly what would happen." She lifted her eyebrows knowingly. "Don't you?"

***

11

Roof deck

Lachlan had laughed and joked with us all day throughout the work. It was almost as though he had always been part of our group.

At some point I'd even given him an easy out, reminding him that he really didn't have to stay and that maybe he had other plans.

But he'd reasoned that since he was missing Christmas at home himself, this was the next best thing.

And then he took over bagging souvenir keychains into little gold satchels for me.

Then again as previously stated, he was a pretty great guy.

The only person who maybe needed a little more convincing was Spencer. But of course, Spencer had a different type of hang-up.

Ever since the server incident and Stella's constantly singing him praises, it seemed Spencer's manhood was just a little bit threatened. He had been trying to one-up Lachlan all day.

Whether in how many boxes he could pack flat in ten minutes, or how fast he could unload the pallets of tree decorations, or how many Die Hard movie quotes he could recite off the top of his head.

I supposed it was Spencer's twisted way of proving himself as worthy as the guy who had won Wanda Meyers' affections.

Ignoring the potential fact that maybe Wanda was the one not worthy of the guy's affections in the first place.

He's too good for Wanda. She's sticking her tongue down some random jock's throat right now. It is up to you.

I shook Stella's words out of my head.

I would go as far as admitting that yes, of course, I liked Lachlan.

But only in the sense that I enjoyed his sense of humor or that I admired his work ethic.

Not because of how ecstatic he'd made me feel when he praised my rudimentary video presentation, calling it a festive Christmas masterpiece.

Besides, I couldn't give up on Jason now. I had been waiting and looking forward to finally seeing him again after all this time. What were a couple more days?

So—new plan.

I just had to make sure to avoid working too closely with Lachlan for the rest of today, and by Sunday, I'd be back home and totally over all this.

That shouldn't be too hard, right?

"Wow, Stella. It's so beautiful," I remarked with a wondrous smile from beneath her perch on top of a ladder.

Stella was arranging several more boughs of holly onto the branches of the big tree. "Astrid and the others did a great job," she noted, pleased. "We're just putting the cherry on top, so to speak."

"Stella!" Spencer's voice rang out from way across the room where he, Pete, and Lachlan were constructing an archway of wreaths by the door.

"What?" Stella's face crumpled.

Spencer was sifting through the contents of some boxes around his feet. "I think we ran out of lights over here."

Pete was holding up one end of a string of blinking lights, standing on top of a step ladder himself. "I'm sure I got all of them out of storage."

"Well, this thing isn't going to reach that thing over there and we can't move those things because it's already looped around. We'd have to redo the whole—Stella!" Spencer yelled out again.

"Whaaat?" Stella paused with a fake green bough in her hand.

I glanced from one to the other, trying to follow their conversation then happened to meet Lachlan's gaze.

He seemed as amused as I was while holding Pete's step-ladder steady for him. He mocked rolling his eyes and I couldn't help a chuckle.

Spencer snapped his fingers. "I think Mom used some of them on the roof deck for last Thanksgiving's party. Could you go grab it?"

Stella scoffed in annoyance. "I'm kind of busy here, doofus."

"Hey, I'll go get it," I volunteered before the sibling rivalry and name-calling could inevitably escalate.

Lachlan jumped over. "I'll come with."

I tried to wave him back. "Oh, you don't have to."

"No, no." He shook his head, already a few steps ahead of me headed for the outdoor stairwell. "Happy to help."

"Oh, okay."

I was puzzled at his eagerness but when we arrived at the top of the stairwell and he pushed open the door, he turned to explain first.

"Um, sorry about that," he apologized. "I was starting to feel a little bit uncomfortable in there. Stella's brother doesn't like me very much, does he?"

I stifled my laughter as it was pretty much as I had suspected. "Don't worry about Spencer," I dismissed. "He's just quirky like that."

As soon as we emerged onto the roof deck, I spotted the twinkly strands of lights right away. They were still entwined around the outdoor trellis.

"Oh boy, I think I found the fairy lights," I announced with a grimace.

We would have to untangle every individual strand of lights from the wooden beams before we could bring them inside.

Lachlan approached the trellis by the marble balustrade but the view stopped him first.

The treetops and low buildings were all covered in white as far as we could see and with the sun barely peeking through the low, gray clouds, casting its faint orange light upon everything, it gave the town a quaint sort of glow despite the dreary weather.

"Wow, look at this."

I smiled, coming up behind him. "Yeah, you know, you can almost see campus from here."

I cast a glance around the exposed deck. Everything was covered under a few inches of snow. All of the furniture had been stored inside and out of the weather.

Lachlan blew out his breath after a moment. "I think it got even colder just now."

I rubbed my hands together. "Yeah."

"I guess we'd better get started. Here, hand me that end." He gestured and we began to take turns catching the ends of the light strands to coil the wires into a neat circle instead of a big tangled mess.

It was tedious work, made even more so as I was still trying not to get too close to him but it was like he was everywhere. It also wasn't helping how warm he felt whenever he brushed against me.

I caught his gaze dart up at me a few times before averting away. He looked even more uncomfortable than I was—no matter what Stella seemed to think.

Then my fingers grazed his for like the tenth time, sending tingles all the way up my arm again despite the cold.

Lachlan cleared his throat to speak up, his tone all casual. "Hey, so...that was great back there." He gestured back toward the closed door. "I mean what you did with Chloe."

That made me laugh and it broke the ice a little. "Oh, you mean when I saved you from having to flirt with the caterer chick? You know you really should be more careful. Some of these girls mean business."

That made his cheeks flush red and he dropped his gaze,

self-conscious, even as his tone was defensive. "I'm sure I would have been able to handle it."

I shot him a skeptical look but didn't want to bruise his ego any further so all I said was, "Right."

"But uh, thanks for stepping in." There was an amused little gleam in his eyes. "It was a very interesting insight into a different side of your personality."

My eyes widened in derision. "Please. I was totally channeling literally anyone else other than myself. Didn't you hear how ridiculous I sounded?" I let out a self-deprecating chuckle. "Like I would ever, ever call someone 'babe'."

He grinned but he tilted his head, meeting my gaze evenly. "I don't know. I kind of like the sound of...'baby.'"

His voice had assumed some husk when he said the word that shivers went up my spine and I was pretty sure I wouldn't mind him calling me that either.

But I forced the thought out of my mind, handing him my end of the string of lights again. "Here."

He glanced over at me as if hesitating to ask something. "You know, I've been thinking about you—what you said yesterday."

"Oh?"

"About integrity?"

"Oh." I cringed, remembering just such the ranting speech. I really hadn't meant to tell him off. "Sorry about that. That was seriously one of the rarer moments that I'm ever high-horsed."

"No, I think you might have been right." His smile had a shy tinge to it. "You know, that maybe just because I can score free chocolate sticks all the time doesn't mean I should."

I was already nodding. "Well," I had to amend after a short pause. "Maybe for chocolate sticks."

Lachlan laughed, his gaze not leaving my face. "They are pretty delicious..." And for the briefest of split seconds, I thought his gaze dropped to my mouth.

I blinked, unable to help a gasp as I stepped back, looking away. "Oh, could you get the last one?" I gestured to the end of the string of lights. "We really should get back inside."

"Yeah." He was concentrating on looping the string of lights around his hands as he walked.

I shifted the other two sets of lights we had already rolled up along my arm and followed behind him.

But just as Lachlan went to turn the doorknob, he jumped back with a start, hissing out a string of half-curses.

"Whoa." I hurried over, already frowning in concern. "What is it?"

"Oh, nothing, the doorknob's stuck and it's freaking frozen," he relayed, gritting his teeth in annoyance, still wringing his hand.

I grimaced, dismissing the sudden urge to take his hand to inspect it for frostbite. Instead, I retrieved my scarf from my pocket to hand it to him. "Here. Maybe try this on the doorknob."

But after a few attempts, Lachlan dropped his arms in exasperation. "Nope. It still won't budge. There's not enough grip."

I blew out a breath, shifting on my feet, looping the scarf around my neck. "Well, this is just great. It's freezing out here." I tugged my sweater closer to my chin.

He set the string of lights down to try the doorknob again,

still hissing in the cold, but snatched his hand away after a few seconds.

Then for some reason, he dropped his head, letting out a half-chuckle groan. "So," he began dryly. "I thought this Christmas was bad but I guess it could always be worse."

"Oh, did you not account for there always being a chance you could freeze to death on a roof deck?" I quipped, setting down the lights I was holding to prop against the side of the door.

His shoulders shook in mirth.

I sighed. "I'm not even supposed to be here right now. I'm supposed to be home in L.A. You know, where you generally don't die of exposure putting up Christmas lights."

I was obviously being facetious but Lachlan's eyes dimmed a bit. "Right." He hesitated. "I suppose you must have had big plans with your family. And...Jasper?" he ventured.

"Jason," I supplied.

He looked away, a sort of smirk on his face. "Sure. You two probably have some sort of Christmas tradition you do every year." He shrugged. "I've observed that often it's the girls who perpetuate the tradition and then they get mad when the guy inevitably forgets."

That made me laugh. "Well then, Jason must have certainly enjoyed being off the hook these last few years."

Lachlan's eyes narrowed. "Huh, what do you mean?"

I made a face. "Well, I actually haven't seen Jason in about six years. We talk on the phone and we're catching up on New Year's but technically, we stopped dating when they moved to Alaska."

Lachlan had stilled.

"What's wrong?"

He blinked, snapping to attention. "Huh? Nothing," he dismissed. "Nothing's wrong." He cleared his throat, averting his gaze again. "Alaska sounds nice."

I gave him a strange look. "Okay...well." I fidgeted in my stance, blowing on my clasped fingers in an attempt to warm myself up. "They'll probably come looking for us soon, right?"

"Let's hope so." He was rubbing his hands together. When he blew out his breath, he happened to peer above the doorway and his eyes narrowed. "Hey, is that a security camera?"

I squinted up at the unnatural shape that could have been a security camera mounted on a metal brace.

It figured that Stella's family must have security cameras all over this place, except this particular camera was covered in about a half-inch layer of frost.

"Not sure how well it works looking like that," I noted.

Lachlan was trying to reach it, grunting as he stretched the length of his entire body. "I can't quite get it."

"Bummer."

He glanced over at me. "Here, I'll lift you."

"What?"

"I think you can reach it if I lift you up. Come over to me."

That beckoning invite sent furious butterflies about in my stomach. He wanted to do what?

I stepped back. "I think um, we should just wait. I'm sure Stella and the guys should be looking for us soon."

He gave me a deadpan look. "Ashleigh, it's freezing out here. This is the fastest way."

A slight bit alarmed, I held my hand out to keep him away.

I couldn't even shake my head vigorously enough in protest. "Seriously, I'm way too heavy. You shouldn't."

Lachlan tilted his head, almost in offense. "This bean pole is stronger than it looks." He urged, "Come on. All you need to do is try to clear the frost off the lens."

I gave him a hesitant, half-panicked look, glancing to the camera, to the frozen door, then back to him, but after a few more seconds of racking my brain and not being able to come up with any more excuses, I let out a haggard, oh-goodness-I-can't-believe-I'm-actually-going-to-do-this sigh.

His eyebrows rose in expectation. "Well?"

I shot him a suffering *alright-already* look, swallowing hard before taking a tentative step forward then another, and as soon as I was close enough, Lachlan braced his hands on my hips to hoist me upward.

I held my breath. I could feel the strength in his hands, his arms, his chest.

Bean pole? Had he been kidding? He was built like a Mack truck.

I didn't want to look down at him in case I completely freaked out. This was so the opposite of trying not to get too close to him. I was already having enough difficulty breathing.

My one hand propped on his ridiculously firm shoulder for balance, I struggled to reach the security camera with the other, struggled to keep focus on my task.

It took quite a few seconds but with the tips of my fingers, I managed to flick the ice off the camera lens.

I blew out a breath. "Got it."

"Good." His voice was half a groan, likely under the strain

of having to lift my entire body weight and he carefully shifted me back down.

Once my feet touched the ground, I had to pause to regain my balance.

But Lachlan didn't pull away.

My heart began pounding when I felt the slightest hint of pressure against my lower back, effectively nudging me just that bit even closer against him.

I pursed my lips, wondering if I had just imagined it. But my brain shut up when I finally braved a glance up at his face.

Lachlan's intense silver eyes were on me, his eyebrows were furrowed and his jaw set.

I immediately flushed and it felt like the middle of summer in my wool layer and cardigan sweater.

Uh-oh.

The shiver running up my spine made me jump away. "Oh," I mumbled, almost stumbling. "Sorry."

He followed me with his stare for a moment, looking breathless himself, but then took the few steps, closing the cold gap between us.

I couldn't help a gasp, couldn't help staring up at him. I was held still by his nearness.

With a sort of marveling in his eyes, Lachlan lifted his hand to brush my hair back from my face, fingertips trailing a whisper down my cheek before his gaze dropped to my mouth again.

"Ashleigh."

His lips drew my attention as he spoke my name and my heart pounded even harder in my chest, in my ears.

If he kissed me, that would be it.

I would probably forget my own name, forget the frigid weather, forget the plain fact that the reason I knew beyond a shadow of a doubt that he was a good kisser was because my roommate had told me so.

Visibly swallowing, Lachlan stroked his thumb across my lower lip and my entire being turned to jelly.

"Feel that?" His voice rumbled in his chest.

I couldn't say no. I didn't want him to stop.

Oh, this was so bad.

My eyes widened in alarm and I staggered back at once, averting my gaze. "We should—we should really... That camera. If we want Stella to see, we should maybe wave or...or..."

I was absolutely not going to open up that can of worms. What did Pete just say about it? I avoided confrontations like the plague.

I was fully prepared to pretend nothing happened since, in fact, nothing did happen.

But Lachlan already knew my move and he wasn't going to let me make it.

His eyebrows were still furrowed, his chest heaving as he assessed, "I thought it was just me. But it isn't, is it?"

It sounded more like a statement than a question and I was sure the deer-caught-in-headlights expression on my face confirmed it too. I dropped my gaze to the ground.

Lachlan moved to approach me again but before he could say anything more, Stella burst through the door.

"What is taking so long, you guys?" She already sounded exasperated.

I spun around, my eyes wide in relief and so much

gratitude. "Stella! Thank goodness. Don't shut that door!" I yelled out. "We're coming in right now."

She looked confused as she watched me pick up the strings of lights from the ground and walk past her before she met Lachlan's gaze. "Is everything okay?"

"Um, that doorknob froze and we couldn't get back in," Lachlan explained as I clattered down the stairs in a rush.

Pete met us halfway across the salon. "Hey, were you out there this whole time? You must be freezing."

"No kidding, Pete." I handed him the string of lights before making a beeline for the giant hearth just before the archway to get warmed up.

Lachlan had done the same thing and gone to stand a few feet to my left, holding his hands out toward the fire. He seemed content not to speak or look at me for the moment.

"Excuse me. The centerpiece flowers go this way, please." Stella had become preoccupied dealing with the many suppliers that were streaming through the entryway to the salon.

It was almost party time.

I checked my wristwatch. "Hey, you guys," I called out. "It's getting pretty late. I should head back now."

Spencer's head popped out from behind a large menorah. "But if you leave now, you'll miss out on our awesome outfits for the party."

I stepped back. "Spencer, I would seriously consider that a bullet well dodged. Besides, I'm sure I'll hear all about it tomorrow. Won't I, Stella?" I yelled out and she met my gaze for a brief moment if only to roll her eyes in displeasure.

Despite everything, I had to stifle my laughter as I stepped back from the mantel.

I gave Lachlan a tentative, prompting look. "You can stay if you like. I'm sure the guys won't mind."

He gave me a small, vague smile. "I'll walk back with you."

"Ashleigh!" Stella called out, leaning over the railing as Lachlan and I descended the stairs. But she only gave me a pointed, meaningful look.

An IOU for an explanation tomorrow.

I waved her away as I put my coat back on and stepped out the door.

The walk back to campus couldn't have been more different from before. Neither Lachlan nor I was talking and the silence was definitely not comfortable.

Snow was falling again and I stuck my hands deeper in my pockets, my stomach still churning in anxiety I thought I might actually be sick.

When I finally spotted the boarding house up the way, just across the street, I had to resist the urge to break into a run and go hide in my room.

I supposed I should have been excited. Stella had been right. There *had* been more than friendliness in Lachlan's manner, more than simple strategic flirting.

Feel that...?

I couldn't stop a warm shiver at the vivid sensations coming back from when he had touched my mouth earlier.

My movement drew Lachlan's concerned gaze. "Are you still cold?"

I shook my head, hunching my shoulders.

"You didn't answer my question."

"No. I'm not cold."

"My other question."

I avoided his gaze. Yeah, like I was going to answer *that* question.

"Look, Ashleigh, we've been doing this dance all day." He raked his hair back with his fingers somewhat in frustration. "And I think I might just explode if I don't get this out."

He stopped walking, turning to face me. "You need to know," he declared, "the past couple of days have been—the brightest spot in what has been a very drab year for me." The exasperated expression on his face softened when he added, "Because of you."

I couldn't look away from the light in his intense gray eyes as they held mine. I couldn't stop the surge of elation in my chest, couldn't stop the smile on my face, I had to bite it back.

One corner of his mouth turned up as he studied my expression. "And when you look at me like that, I can tell you feel something too."

There was a battle of butterflies in my stomach. On the one hand, it was everything I was hoping to hear. On the other, it was the last thing I should be wanting to hear.

But when he moved closer, I jerked away.

"Am I wrong?" His gray eyes dimmed.

I cast mine down. "Look, Lachlan, you're great but..."

"But am I wrong?"

"It's not relevant."

"It's completely relevant!" I exclaimed in frustration. "You're supposed to be with Wanda!"

He shook his head as if in incredulity. "That doesn't matter."

My jaw dropped. "Are you actually kidding me? Do you have some kind of bizarre observational theory about this too? You can flirt with girls to get special treatment. You can charm your way out of anything—"

"No—!" he tried to cut in but I was on a roll.

I gestured to all of him. "I should have known. You've definitely got to be way too smart for your own good if you're even able to rationalize your way out of something like this. How on Earth could you possibly say this doesn't matter?"

He hesitated. "Because—"

"Because what?"

"Because—"

"What?"

"Because I was going to break up with Wanda!"

Stunned at his outburst, I stopped way short. "What?"

Lachlan dropped his hands, blowing out a big sigh. He paused for a second before repeating what he said. "I was going to break up with Wanda." He dropped his gaze to the ground. "That's why I'm here. That's why I came."

My jaw dropped again. He was going to what?

"I didn't want to do it over the phone. But I didn't want to keep doing the long-distance thing anymore."

Given what I knew, I supposed I shouldn't have been shocked.

But Lachlan had always been Wanda's ever-reliable, a fixture in her life, and all this time, I had been led to believe that despite the quirkiness of their relationship, it was rock solid, and that all of Wanda's overly dramatic complaints were just that.

And if I was shocked by the news, Wanda was so totally going to freak the heck out.

I began to shake my head in indignation. "Don't. You shouldn't. Wanda—she really cares about you."

Lachlan was in stark disbelief. "You can't possibly believe that!"

I shot him a mocking look. "Why not?"

"Where *is* Wanda?" He gave me a skeptical glare. "Right now, huh? You know exactly where she is, right? She'd rather be anywhere else but with me right now. She's avoiding me. She is, isn't she?"

"I can't really—"

"Is Wanda avoiding me? It's a simple question, Ashleigh." He threw his hands up. "Yes or no?"

It was anything but a simple question. I pursed my lips, feeling helpless. I couldn't tell him what he wanted to hear and I definitely couldn't tell him what he didn't want to hear.

Lachlan grunted in irritation, gesturing back down the road. "And everyone back there already knew, didn't they?" He curled his lips. "Your friends all probably think I'm such a chump, waiting around for Wanda like a pathetic lap dog. Well, you know what? I *was* a pathetic lap dog. And the only good thing Wanda's really done for me was to make me realize I didn't have to be one."

He closed his eyes for a moment as though to collect himself from his outburst. "Honestly, I've been dreading having to talk to Wanda all week. I would have just left too but..." He reached for my hand, his touch sending tingles up and down my arm. "I didn't expect this."

He gave me a little tug to pull me closer, his smile widening when I didn't resist.

My heart pounded in my chest in anxiety. I was indescribably happy to hear that Lachlan felt the same way about me. But the fact that I *was* happy just distressed me even more.

Emotionally drained, my gaze was off to one side. "I don't want to hurt her."

Lachlan's smile quirked a little. "That still doesn't answer my question."

I shot him a wry, incredulous look. Goodness, if he still didn't know the answer to his darn question. "No, Lachlan. It's not just you."

And despite the freezing cold winter's evening, it was like the sun rose in his eyes.

He was heaving in exhilaration, in relief. "I love hearing you say my name," he whispered, leaning closer, cupping my face in one hand.

But I braced my hand on his chest to stop him. "Wait." I struggled to keep a level head. "I still think you should clear things up with Wanda first. Before—before you..."

His gaze was pinned to my mouth, his voice a low husky rumble. "Before I can kiss you...?"

I drew in a haggard deep breath before I became completely mesmerized and stepped away so there were at least three feet of space between us.

Lachlan took a moment to even out his own breathing. Then he tilted his head to give me an amused look through a strained chuckle. "You're a really good friend. Wanda's really lucky."

Gosh. If only she knew *how* lucky.

We crossed the street and he led me up the steps of the boarding house.

When I turned to Lachlan at the door to say goodbye, there was another catch in his enigmatic smile. "I had a really good time with you today."

"Even when we almost froze to death taking down those lights?" I couldn't help but quip.

He nodded. "Especially then."

I couldn't stop smiling so widely, my face was beginning to hurt. "I'll see you tomorrow."

"I can't wait..."

Another shiver coursed through me at the timbre of his voice—deep, rich, full of promise.

He'd started to turn to leave but he paused in mid-stride. "Hey, Ash," he called out, his eyebrows slightly furrowed. "Could you do me a favor and don't tell Wanda yet about...you know? I really think it needs to come from me."

I pursed my lips, nodding in agreement. I had to admit I was also a bit impressed that he was willing to be accountable and face Wanda himself.

I watched him walk away, almost in wonder myself, and again elation, and then again distress.

As soon as Lachlan had disappeared around the corner, I trudged through the doorway and collapsed with a huge sigh into one of the plush chairs in the receiving room.

My brain was a puddle with too many thoughts to process. My spirits soared with all kinds of happy, new possibilities about being with Lachlan but also I couldn't stop thinking about how Wanda would react to the news—*all* the news.

I wanted to cross my fingers hoping she would be so

enamored over Doug now, she wouldn't even care but it was hard to tell with Wanda sometimes.

And what about Jason? I was seeing him in like three days. What if he actually did want to get back together? He might totally think I'd been leading him on all this time.

I groaned, sinking back deeper into the chair, closing my eyes for a moment. I didn't hear a door creak open and slam shut, and when I opened my eyes again, Yvette's dour face was already peering down at me.

"So I guess you must have a great personality if you managed to bag a guy that hot 'cause it's certainly not from your looks."

As usual, it seemed Yvette had nothing better to do than to mess with me, and too, she must have been watching Lachlan and me talking at the door from her creepy window.

Except today, I was too mentally exhausted to play her little mind games so when she snickered and poked at my shoulder, I surprised both of us by jumping up and whirling around to yell, "Jeez, Yvette! Read the bloody room! Not now!"

Yvette's face was a picture of shock, her eyes wide, her mouth hanging open. She was so completely taken aback, she couldn't say anything else.

And for the first time, without anyone else's saying so, she actually turned around to leave me alone.

12

The Reverse

"How much do you hate me right now?"

Wanda's doleful eyes popped up above the paperback I was reading.

I thought I had finally gotten lucky this morning. Nobody else was in the sunroom when I'd come in to read. I thought I'd finally have some peace and quiet.

Or maybe just quiet.

I wasn't entirely sure about the peace part since now I was trying to hide several giant secrets.

I'd made sure I was indisposed by the time Wanda had come home from her date last night and I'd gotten up insanely early to have breakfast just so I would avoid the inevitable interrogation.

But Wanda found me anyway. She was still wearing her dressing robe, her hair only half-brushed. Only something urgent could have made her get up in such a state to look for me.

I almost worried that somehow Wanda had gotten wind of everything.

But I was familiar enough with the looks on her face that I could tell Wanda was trying to absolve her own guilt this time, instead of trying to assign blame.

"How bad was it?" Wanda straightened up, already cringing as she began to pace back and forth in front of my nose. "I am so sorry I had to leave you like that yesterday. It's just Doug totally caught me by surprise and I got carried away."

She blew out an exasperated breath, smacking her palm on her forehead. "Oh, I am such a bad friend. I swear I will never, ever do anything like that to you ever again."

But inwardly, I was cringing too. "Settle down," I had to say so she'd finally quit pacing. "It was fine. Nothing happened."

Nothing happened.

Nothing happened.

Wanda turned to me again, her eyes wide in relief and gratitude. "Oh, thank you so much! You have no idea how terrible I felt. Thank you so much for keeping Locky company." She nodded once in approval. "He said you were firm but fair."

My ears perked up. "He said what?"

"Oh, I called him last night to apologize again and he said you let him tag along to Stella's and ordered him around all day."

My heart nearly stopped. "Oh. Right. That. Sure."

"He said he had a blast hanging out with you guys and that Stella's house was super amazing." She rolled her eyes. "Like we didn't already know that, right?" she joked.

My chuckle was strained.

"Anyway." She let out an overly dramatic sigh. "Locky's coming over again later today. It's just a good thing he's such a soft touch. Believe me, I honestly thought he would have just straight-up left town. I'm so glad you convinced him to stay.

My chest constricted at that. "Yeah. Good for me." I mocked a cheer, curling my lips.

Wanda giggled, playfully smacking my arm. "Now close that book and come upstairs. You absolutely have to help me find something extra special to wear." She gestured to the front desk. "I'll just go tell Becca that I'm expecting him. I want to make sure I don't miss him this time."

My stomach churning, I watched Wanda approach the desk. She looked so happy. She had zero idea that Lachlan was actually planning to break up with her.

Granted, she wasn't entirely the most virtuous person I knew but she was my friend. My chest pained when I imagined the look on her face when he told her it was over.

But when Yvette came into view, strolling into the sun-room, all my anxieties were erased altogether. All except one.

She had a curious, wary look in her eyes, sizing me up as if trying to gauge if last night's decidedly extraordinary inter-action was a complete fluke.

But I squared my shoulders and prepared to walk right past her.

Of course, she couldn't help it.

"Hey." She grabbed my shoulder.

I was going to push away but her next question caught me off guard.

"How's your boyfriend?"

I blinked. "I beg your pardon?"

Yvette narrowed her eyes and I really should have given my response a bit more thought given its implications, not to mention what someone like Yvette might do with the information when she asked, "That guy you went out with yesterday."

But my automatic, almost already defensive answer was, "Oh, he's not my boyfriend. He's Wanda's boyfriend."

I knew I'd made a mistake when Yvette's dark eyes lit up as obviously, to anyone not previously briefed of the situation, a scandal must be brewing.

I wanted to refute it but my heart pounded in my chest upon hearing myself how it must have sounded like and more to the point, how accurate her unknowing, casual suspicion actually was.

"Oh, really?" Yvette's drawl rolled her r's as she broke a sly grin, already glancing over at the desk where Wanda was happily chatting to Becca.

Yvette nudged me with her shoulder—hard. "I wonder what your little friend would do if she found out you were going out with her boyfriend behind her back."

I glared at Yvette. Was she seriously trying to blackmail me now?

I shot a look over toward the desk myself and happened to catch Wanda's gaze.

She was frowning as she watched us from afar, no doubt already guessing that Yvette was up to no good over here.

But Wanda just motioned a short nod at me, quirking her eyebrows up in silent encouragement.

Stay strong. You can do this.

I took a beat, puffing up my chest before turning my glare back onto Yvette. "You know what I wonder?" I prompted. "I wonder what the Office would do if I file a peer dispute complaint against you for all the bullying you do to me every day."

Yvette's face blanked.

"It probably wouldn't look good to lose your so-called 'good standing' on your permanent college file." I put my finger up in conjecture. "Oh, but I bet you've already thought of that, haven't you? Because you're so smart."

Yvette stepped back in revulsion at the same time that Wanda arrived to pull me away and she flashed Yvette a sweet smile and a wave.

"*Adios*, Yvette."

I broke a relieved smile as Wanda and I took up the stairs. A lump was still in my throat but man, did that feel fantastic.

Wanda was squealing. "That look on her face. You gave it to her good!" she exclaimed. "Do you see what comes from taking my advice?"

I rolled my eyes but had to hand it to her. Nobody else in the world nagged me to death more about standing up for myself than Wanda.

"Oh, I wish I'd heard every word you guys said," she added as we got to our room.

And my smile faded in an instant.

Fortunately, Wanda was preoccupied, struggling to shove our door wider when it kept catching on an old sweater on the floor.

I bent over to pick it up. "Seriously, Wanda," I started, matter-of-factly. "You need to pick up your clothes." I tossed the sweater onto her bed, on top of an already piled-up mess of clothes.

Wanda grimaced, picking up the garment. "Seriously, Ashleigh. That is *your* sweater." And she tossed it back at my face.

That made me laugh as it dropped in my hands and I made my way to my bed, sitting down and folding said sweater.

"Hey," she piped up, her eyes bright. "I never even got to tell you what the surprise was that Doug wanted to show me yesterday."

I didn't know why Wanda thought I would even be remotely interested in what Doug found noteworthy enough to qualify as a surprise for a girl he was dating.

But Wanda forged on with great enthusiasm. "Doug had had his car wrapped in that shiny vinyl thing—you know the one in those ads on TV? Then we went for a drive up the coast." She shook her head, her gaze faraway. "I'd forgotten how beautiful it is out there, even in wintertime."

"Okay." I pulled out another sweater that I had been sitting on to start folding that too.

She let out a dreamy sigh before wading over to her closet then asking offhand, "So where do you think Locky and I should go today? I'm thinking it should be somewhere special."

A sharp twinge in my chest made me grimace. It bothered me how quickly Wanda had just changed gears.

Bothered me a lot.

And I was really hating the idea that she was only seeing Lachlan like an old standby after being done with her flashy, new boy toy.

Lachlan surely deserved way more than that.

I tried to bite my tongue.

Don't say it. Don't say it.

Nope.

"Why are you even still with him?" I couldn't help but ask.

Wanda stopped short. "Who, Locky?" She tilted her head, sending her thoughts back into the clouds and I immediately regretted asking my question.

"Oh, Locky's just so…" She let out another sigh. "He's just such a nice guy, you know? And he's so sweet. And he's whip-smart, like, you have no idea." Her eyes widened in emphasis. "And you wouldn't know it when you look at him, and I know I've probably told you about a million times but he's just such a good kisser!"

I closed my eyes for a moment, ignoring the sudden pounding in my head and I buried my face in a pillow.

"Don't even get me started on his eyes and that smile—"

"Alright!" I cut in, throwing my hands up. "Wanda, feel free to shut up anytime."

She stood confused, hands on hips. "What? Now you hate Locky and you want me to break up with him?"

"I just—want to make absolutely sure that, you know, he ticks all your boxes…?" I rationalized with a shrug. "Otherwise—otherwise, you know, you should put him out of his misery."

I gestured with my hand. "I mean, come on. You should have seen the look on his face yesterday morning. He was so disappointed when you didn't turn up."

"Aww," Wanda cooed. "Well, don't you worry. I'm totally going to make it up to him today. What's something totally romantic you think we should do?"

Oh, perfect. The last conversation I wanted to have right now. "I don't know, Wanda." I slumped back in bed.

"Well, you have to help me!" She tugged on the pillow I was using to cover my head. "This could be my last chance. I don't want to lose him."

I propped up on my elbows, giving her a leveled curious look at her sort of dramatic, ominous statement. She was making it sound like it was suddenly a life or death situation.

"Wanda, is there something else going on?"

I knew Wanda was a big flirt. She had been drooling over Doug all year. And I'd thought she had been avoiding Lachlan because she was exactly that—a big flirt, drooling over Doug all year.

But the hesitant look on Wanda's face seemed to hint at something else, something deeper.

She looked away for a moment. "It's just..." she started, her forehead creased. "When I first met Locky, he could barely even look at me. But I knew his confidence was just hiding beneath the surface. He had so much going for him, I wanted him to realize that and be proud of himself."

I slowly sat up in bed, almost stunned. This was a part of their story that she had never shared with me before.

"Now he's not that timid, easy to impress guy anymore." She turned an imploring look at me. "What if now he's disappointed in me?"

My mouth dropped open. Oh jeez, Wanda was actually worried about what Lachlan thought of her.

"He's always kept me real, you know?" She fidgeted with the edges of my bedsheet. "I mean if a decent guy like him can like me...maybe I'm not such a big hoe who can only get dumb jocks."

That statement struck a serious chord in me as apparently, underneath her self-assured façade, Wanda was just as much insecure as everyone else.

The funny thing though was that whether or not she and Lachlan both knew it, they had already changed each other for the better.

I took a deep breath with a sinking realization. Wanda and Lachlan needed each other. He *really* was important to her.

And now he was about to break her heart.

And—oh, crap—I wasn't going to let him, was I?

My stomach churned in remorse.

I was the third wheel here. The two of them had history. Their relationship didn't deserve to fall apart just because of my stupid, little, meaningless crush.

I was the one who had to step back.

Even if...

My heart jumped to my throat when the phone rang.

"No! Is he here?" Wanda started throwing clothes all over the place. "I'm not ready yet! Get the phone, Ash!"

Too flustered to contest her instruction, I shifted over to pick up the phone.

Wanda was wide-eyed, watching me (instead of finishing getting dressed, by the way) random articles of clothing clutched to her chest.

But when I heard who was on the phone, I had to roll my eyes and held the receiver out to her. "It's your dad."

She blinked. "Oh."

Her parents rarely called her. They were sort of "hands-off" parents which in hindsight was probably one of the main causes of Wanda's likely deeply-rooted insecurity.

I sagged back in bed and looked out the window, frowning when I noticed more white flakes sailing down from the sky.

I was hoping the weather had settled down fairly enough that my flight wouldn't get canceled again.

I'd seriously had enough of this in-school Christmas vacation.

Like it was fate, I spotted the familiar top of the head of a tall guy walking down the sidewalk and turning toward our building.

"Lachlan is here." I gestured out the window, unable to muster enough strength to speak louder than a whisper.

But Wanda had heard me and she let out a helpless groan.

For literally anybody else, she would have just hung up the phone. But this was 'Daddy'—whose main produce was Wanda's allowance.

She covered the bottom of the receiver and hissed at me, her expression pleading. "Could you please—?"

Of course.

Why the heck not?

After reminding Wanda that I was in fact, not her slave, I headed downstairs.

I easily spotted Lachlan in the lobby, about to approach the desk to ask Becca to page Wanda.

I almost stumbled at the sight of him.

Why on Earth did he have to be so cute anyway? Why couldn't he ever have one bad hair day if only to make me feel better about what I now had to do?

The brightest spot in what has been a very drab year...because of you.

But I shook my head to clear those confusing thoughts.

He's important to Wanda. You've never seen Wanda so worked up about any guy ever before, I reminded myself firmly before calling out. "Hey."

Lachlan looked up in the direction of my voice and his face lit up like it was Christmas morning again and my heart jumped unexpectedly.

His eager smile as he approached me faltered when he remembered that he was still supposed to keep his distance and the light in his eyes dimmed a little.

He looked away for a second, cracking his neck in tempered frustration. "Is Wanda upstairs? Or is this you coming down to give me another excuse?"

If I wasn't so tense, I would have laughed.

"No," I told him. "She's actually upstairs."

"She's really coming this time?"

"Yes." I swallowed hard. "And she's really looking forward to seeing you. Really."

Lachlan peered at my face. "So...you didn't tell her."

I pursed my lips. "You said not to."

"I said a lot of things."

My chest constricted again but I was already resolved to get through this. "Listen, about that..." I let out a strained sigh. "Wanda really wants this to work with you and I think... I think you should hear her out."

He had to stifle back a chuckle. "You are so loyal to her."

I shook my head. "No, listen—"

"But I think that just makes me like you even more." And

there went that charming smile again. "I was up all night thinking about seeing you again today. I barely slept."

"Lachlan—"

His grin turned lopsided. "You have no idea how badly I've been wanting to—"

"Lachlan, shut up for a second," I hissed.

He blinked, his eyebrows furrowing. "What's going on?"

I kept shaking my head. "I can't—we can't—you can't—you can't break up with her."

"What?"

I winced, turning to leave. "I'm sorry but I don't think we should do this."

"Wait, Ash, I—"

"Locky!" Wanda's sweet purr floated down the stairs right then and we both turned to look.

Wanda looked radiant in her scoop-neck sweater and tailored pants and she had fixed up her hair in a soft bun with wispy tendrils framing her face. She wasn't kidding when she said wanted to look extra special today.

When I saw the completely entranced look on Lachlan's face, I couldn't even blame him. He did say he'd always been in awe of her.

I glanced down at my jeans and oversized cardigan sweater, unable to help but compare. If it wasn't before, Lachlan's choice should be crystal clear now.

I took a deep breath, forcing a smile. "And you finally meet."

I should have been satisfied. This was exactly what I'd wanted to happen. For them to give each other and their relationship another chance. This was exactly what should have happened right from the start before I even got involved.

"I've missed you so much. I love your coat," Wanda cooed as she took Lachlan's arm and leaned up to kiss his cheek.

This was my cue to leave.

"Well, I'll see you guys later." I waved goodbye to Wanda, not strong enough just then to meet Lachlan's gaze, and headed straight out the door.

13

Panic at the Cafe

In my fluster, I'd forgotten to grab my jacket and would actually have been really cold if it wasn't for all the nervous adrenaline pumping through my veins as I fast-walked to The Sweet Corner where I knew my friends would be.

I made a beeline to that window booth like it was a beacon. I seriously needed something to take my mind off of all this drama and I was sure they would oblige.

"Hey, Ash," Pete greeted as I arrived.

I shoved him aside to make space for me to sit down. "Hey, guys, what's up?"

Stella gave my woolly cardigan a once-over. "Where's your jacket?"

"I forgot to bring it," I dismissed, not willing to get into why and changing the subject immediately. "So how was the party?"

Pete guffawed. "We totally pulled off the pastel suits! I told you it would be a winner."

Stella rolled her eyes.

"Yeah." Spencer elbowed Stella as he stirred his coffee. "Dad didn't even seem to mind it at all."

"Obviously you weren't watching Mom's reaction." She turned to her boyfriend. "Seriously Pete, you already know you started on thin ice with Mom ever since that Ming vase incident."

"What, your mom loves me now," Pete insisted with a grin. "Anyway, it really was such a shame you didn't stick around, Ash. It was definitely a night to remember."

"Oh, I think Ash had way more important things to do last night." Stella winked.

Pete had begun to stuff his face with pie. "Like what?"

Spencer however was concerned about other things, craning his neck behind me toward the door. "Is Wanda with you?"

"She's with her boyfriend," I replied.

At the flatness of my tone, Stella almost choked on her milkshake, giggling afterward. "Oh my gosh, Ash."

I narrowed my eyes at her. "Hah. Serves you right." I reached over to steal some wafers off of her parfait. "I'm figuring they need some quality time together—"

She smacked my hand away. "Hey!"

"Hey!" Pete piped up. "Speaking of quality parties, I just heard about this New Year's Eve bash at the Alpha Kappa house."

"Yeah!" Spencer cheered, giving him a high-five. "Another place for fancy dress."

Stella let out a long-suffering sigh before casting me a prompting glance. "Ash, wanna come?"

"Can't. My flight leaves on Sunday. And I gotta say, I'm so relieved." I made a wide-eyed face in emphasis. "I can't wait to get back home where there's none of this stupid snow and stupid drama."

The bell over the door jangled and I looked up.

Wanda and Lachlan.

Of course.

I made a face in disapproval first before my panic.

Wanda had been mulling over all these special plans for her and Lachlan's special reunion all day and then decided to bring him here? The most ordinary place on campus?

"Hey, Wanda!" Pete called out. "Lachlan, how's the man?"

"Hey guys," Wanda flashed a bright smile at everyone as they approached our booth. "Locky, I think you've met everyone?"

Stella and Spencer chimed in a greeting.

I wasn't paying attention. I was busy picking more stuff off of Stella's parfait while she was distracted, not particularly keen to meet anyone else's gaze.

Lachlan cleared his throat. "Well, I guess it's pretty crowded there," he noted of our table with a catch in his tone.

"No, no." Stella eagerly shook her head. "Just budge your big butt over, Spencer." She shooed him back and Pete got up to sit at the other end of the booth—effectively making Lachlan sit beside me with Wanda at his other side.

Seriously.

Lachlan shifted in his seat before giving me an uncertain side glance. "Hey."

My reply was short. "Hi."

I was sure he was still confused about what I'd said earlier but since he had come here with Wanda, he must have decided against breaking up with her after all.

"So should we order?" Wanda asked Lachlan, looping her arm through his.

"Order for Ash too, would you?" Stella spoke up in irritation, snatching her nearly bald parfait back away from me.

I shot her a sheepish look.

"Oh, of course." Wanda rolled her eyes, knowingly. "Miss, what can I get for you today?" she mocked a waitress' dulcet tone.

"Maybe she wants what you're having," Stella quipped.

I shot Stella a snarly look. *Jeez!* But of course, Wanda hadn't noticed and I forced a grin back up at her. "Just get me a spiced pudding cake, please. Thanks."

And when the happy couple headed for the counter, I reached over to smack Stella's arm. "What are you trying to do?"

She beamed at me. "What does it look like? I'm trying to force you to do something you already know you want to."

I let out a haggard sigh. I knew I owed Stella a bit of clarification but I didn't have the time or the mental stamina to explain everything to her right now as the situation had gotten quite a bit more complicated.

"Wow," Pete began, concerned about something else. "Is it me or does this place seem a bit more packed today?"

"Maybe a lot more people are back from vacation already," Spencer suggested, turning in his seat to watch the incoming crowd.

Then it struck me how dangerous it actually was here—for Wanda.

The Sweet Corner was literally every college student's hang-out. I would hate to imagine what would happen if Doug and his friends suddenly arrived.

Chaos, probably.

When Wanda and Lachlan came back to the table, she set the little plate in front of me. "Here you go."

"Thanks."

Lachlan shifted into the booth beside me before Wanda slid in, and when Lachlan set his Christmas milkshake down, without my saying so, or moving anywhere remotely near him, he began to pick out a couple of marshmallows off it and set them on the side of my plate.

I stiffened at the strange constriction in my chest. It was such a sweet gesture but of course, I had to pretend I hadn't noticed.

Stella noticed though and she met my gaze—pointedly yet again.

I tried to ignore her.

Pete and Spencer were preoccupied gathering coins on the table, preparing to head for the jukebox.

"Hey, Carrie! I didn't know you were back yet." Wanda popped back out of her seat to cross the aisle to chat with a friend.

I stuffed the marshmallows into my mouth before anyone else noticed, pretending the whole thing hadn't happened before I cut into my cake.

But I frowned right away as the dry, crumbly morsels flaked off my fork.

Lachlan noticed my pause again. "What is it?"

I pursed my lips. "Nothing. It's fine."

"Oh boy, here we go again," he mumbled.

Stella was watching me too. "Ash, for the millionth time, if they gave you the wrong thing, just send it back."

"It's no big deal," I insisted. "They just gave me the vegan pudding instead of the good one. But I can have it, seriously. I really shouldn't be picky about this type of stuff."

Lachlan took the fork away from me. "Are you going to tell me you can live without cake too?"

His face was full mocking, I couldn't help my mirth. "No. You stay out of this."

"What?" He feigned innocence. "I just happen to think that you shouldn't simply keep settling for what you're offered."

"Sometimes you have to take what you want, Ash," Stella interjected, her tone all pointed.

My mouth dropped open as I looked between Lachlan and Stella. "It's seriously fine, guys." I reached for the fork again.

"No, it's not," Lachlan argued. "Ash, you need to send it back."

"Look, I can eat it, see—?" I cut into the cake again.

But he caught my hand to stop me. "No, you need to send it back."

"I'm telling you it's fine," I insisted, trying to push him back even as he kept yanking away my hand holding the fork.

"Ashleigh, you know we're right, come on." He had braced one arm around me to make sure I couldn't take a bite and at one point, he tugged too hard, almost hoisting me onto his lap and bringing my face a mere inches in front of his.

Lachlan froze in place, looking surprised himself, and for

a moment, all I could do was stare back into his challenging eyes.

Feel that...?

A warm shiver coursed right through me and I winced, this time managing to easily push away as Lachlan let me go.

I cleared my throat, casting Stella's entirely amused expression a side glance, but Lachlan was still giving me an expectant look.

I let out an exasperated groan. "Fine! I'll do it already." I returned his pointed look as I raised my hand to call the nearest wait staff.

I wasn't quite sure about the real reason for my heart pounding and I was pretty sure I stammered all through it but like everyone else but I expected, my request went through to the kitchen without any untoward incidents.

Stella's jaw was unhinged as she merely watched without a word. She tugged on Pete's sleeve just as the guys walked back. "Ashleigh just sent her food back."

"What?" Spencer's eyes were wide.

"Dude." Pete slapped my back in congratulations.

I watched the waitress place the new plate of cake in front of me and I was thanking her just as Wanda came back to the table.

"What the heck just happened? Did you actually just send your food back?" She turned her awed expression toward me.

Lachlan was smirking to himself, looking pleased but he didn't say anything.

"Well, this is a momentous occasion," Wanda cheered, giving everyone at the table a meaningful look. "You guys, do you know what else? This morning, I swear I saw Ash stand up to that beeyatch Yvette back at the dorms who's been bullying all year."

"No kidding." Stella's jaw dropped again.

And Lachlan gave me a surprised look too. "No kidding."

I flushed, dropping my gaze. "Alright, alright, everyone stop staring at me already." I put a forkful of cake in my mouth to have an excuse not to go on.

Wanda leaned across Lachlan's lap to throw her arms around my shoulders. "I'm so proud of you!"

Oh, perfect.

14

Doug

The bell over the café door jangled again.

I must have already been on high alert with all the secrets I'd been trying to keep lately. Except for me, nobody else noticed Doug Taylor and a couple of his friends come in.

For all that I shouldn't care and that it really had nothing to do with me anyway, I still jumped up and dragged Wanda off to the ladies' room post-haste.

"What's the big idea, Ashleigh?" she demanded as soon as I'd closed the door behind us. "Isn't it usually me that holds these covert meetings in the ladies' room?"

"Yeah, so sorry to break the tradition," I hissed. "But Doug Taylor just came in."

"Doug?" She made a face. "So? I'm not into him anymore."

I waved in her face, unable to believe how dense she was being right then. "Uh, hello, Wanda? Do you not see how potentially catastrophic the situation is?"

I gave her a pointed look, motioning discrete imaginary boxes in the air. "Doug. Lachlan. You. All in the same place at the same time? Ring any kind of alarm bells? I don't suppose you've told them about each other, have you?"

Wanda actually appeared to give it some thought before it finally dawned on her. "Oh my gosh, you're right. Um, okay. Look, I'll just have to—" She stammered, "I'll-I'll sneak out and you get Lachlan to come and meet me outside at the parking lot."

"Me? Wanda, I am not going to get in the middle of—"

Protests were obviously pointless as Wanda cut mine off. "Thanks, sweetie. You're a pal." She gave me a quick hug and disappeared out the door.

"Aagh!" I groaned in exasperation but here I was again, having been left no choice.

When I trudged back to our table, Stella was trying to meet my gaze and her eyes told me she had finally noticed Doug too.

I gave her a slight nod in acknowledgment before sitting back down as calmly as I could to execute the plan.

I turned to Lachlan. "Hey." I laid my hand on his forearm.

Lachlan looked over at me in surprise and he broke a ridiculously disarming smile. "Hey."

And I completely forgot what I was supposed to do. "Uh..."

It was Spencer who snapped me out of it by asking, "Where's Wanda?"

I jerked up to stand. "Right. That. Lachlan, hey, Wanda said she'd like for you to meet her outside." I gestured to the door.

"Ash, is something wrong?" Lachlan already looked concerned as he grabbed his coat, standing up to follow me.

"No, no," I dismissed. "Wanda just wanted to see you in private, I think." I led him to the other diner's exit.

But halfway there, Lachlan caught my arm first. "Listen, Ashleigh, there's something we need to talk about. About Wanda."

Not looking at him, I tried to swallow the lump in my throat.

No doubt he was going to tell me that he had changed his mind. He was finally happy with Wanda and what had almost happened between us was a total mistake.

"You don't have to explain to me—"

"No, listen." He peered at my face, trying to make me look up at him. "I don't know what happened between you and Wanda this morning but I still have to break up with her." He touched my chin, light as a feather. "And I still want you."

I could feel the warmth from his skin, from his eyes. I hoped mine didn't betray me at the moment.

"Look, Lachlan, I think we just need to forget what happened yesterday," I said as rationally as I could despite his closeness. "You were right, okay? Wanda was trying to avoid you. But not for the reasons you thought. In fact, not even for the reasons *I* thought."

He raked his hair back in frustration. "What is that even supposed to mean?"

"I can explain later," I cut in. "For right now, we have to go outside." I gestured away.

The café door swung open letting in a cold waft hinting at the yet again, frigid conditions outside.

He gave me a once-over. "Hey, you don't even have a jacket."

"Lachlan—" I tried to protest but he nudged me to turn my back so he could put his coat on me.

Except I happened to look out the window just then and my surprised gasp made Lachlan look up too, right in time to see Wanda pull away from Doug.

It was obvious the two of them had just been kissing.

Uh-oh.

Lachlan's eyebrows snapped together and after an unsettling moment, his eyes cleared when the full meaning of what had really been going on finally hit him.

What Wanda had been doing behind his back. What I had been doing for Wanda to hide it.

His mouth dropped open when he met my gaze again but while he couldn't seem to form words, I could see the appalled accusation in his eyes.

Yes, I knew about it. I answered his silent question in my head, feeling sick to my stomach.

Lachlan took a few seconds to collect himself, then he cursed under his breath before plowing through the door and stalking over to the "happy" couple.

I didn't move—couldn't move, didn't even want to watch. I dropped my gaze to my shoes in horror.

Didn't I say exactly this would happen?

I heard angry shouts and a final, "No, Doug!" from Wanda before I looked up to see Lachlan stagger back, his face red as he scowled back at Doug. But whatever had happened, Lachlan didn't move to retaliate.

Wanda had started crying and I finally pushed outside to rush over to her. "Are you okay?"

Doug cast a distasteful glance at each of us down his nose, straightening up the collar of his letter jacket before huffing away with a rude grunt. "Done with that."

My poisonous glare escorted him away down the lane right until Doug turned the corner and was out of sight.

I blew out a breath in relief that the notorious jock hadn't been interested in making any more of the trouble I was most certain he could.

I hesitated before turning to check on Lachlan.

His face was angry. Angry and closed.

"Locky..." Wanda tried to reach him.

Lachlan shrugged her off, shaking his head in disbelief. He wouldn't meet anyone's gaze.

I could see the gears spinning furiously in his head again as if to try to process every aspect of exactly what had just happened.

But after another minute, he muttered, "I don't know what I was thinking," before whirling around to leave.

"Lachlan, wait!" Another pointless call on my part.

Wanda started sobbing harder. "Oh, Ash..."

I blew out another sigh and patted her back.

Oh, Wanda...

15

Solution

"No, no, and no." I couldn't protest hard enough. "I've definitely meddled in your business long enough. I won't do it anymore. I can't and I won't."

I had woken up early to start packing for my flight this evening but instead, I was having to soothe my crazy roommate through one of her bawling fits.

Wanda's eyes were still red and puffy. Her nose was swollen, a tissue crumpled up in her hand as she slumped in her bed.

She'd explained to me how Doug had caught her by surprise with the kiss yesterday and how she wasn't able to pull away fast enough without making a scene.

And this morning, bright and early, she was telling me her brilliant plan to get Lachlan back.

Her perfect solution to everything.

Have me solve it.

"Why me?" I protested, throwing my little toiletry kit into my duffel so hard it landed with a thud.

"Because Locky probably hates me right now. He's not going to want to talk to me!" she complained. "And he was jabbering on and on about how really nice you'd been to him this week so—"

How could I tell her why I was the last person on Earth that should possibly do this for her right now?

But Wanda was adamant. She gave me a pout—something which normally got anyone to do her bidding.

But not me.

I was firm.

I had to be firm.

"Wanda. No."

She came over and bounced onto my bed. "Oh, come on, Ash. Please?" She gave me her most hopeful look. "I am so totally crazy about him."

I shot her a seriously confused look.

"I mean I may have made it sound like I was only feeling sorry for him yesterday because he sort of worshipped the ground I walked on." Wanda's confession turned her a shade of red. "But I think I like him even more now."

I could only gawk at her as I tried to sort out Wanda's clothes from mine from the heap on the bed.

"And I was about to tell Doug, I really was! I mean obviously, I already knew that was never going to work out. But now I am definitely over it," she concluded. "And I want Lachlan."

My eyes lit up and I shot her a surprised look.

"What?"

"You just called him Lachlan," I noted, a lead weight settling on my chest and I dropped my arms.

Wanda was serious.

"Yes," she said through a haggard breath. "You know when they say you don't know what you have until you lose it? Well, I think I do now and I don't want to lose him. Please? Ashleigh?" She gave me that desperate, pleading look again. "It would mean the whole world."

I shook my head, letting out a deep, deep sigh.

Wanda saw my sigh of resignation. "You'll do it?" she cried and threw her arms around me. "Oh, thank you! Thank you! You have absolutely no idea what you're going to do for me."

Well. She was absolutely right about that.

***

Wanda was so happy with me she helped me finish packing. And by that, I meant helped me haphazardly toss several other articles of clothing into my already bursting luggage.

My stomach churned at the look of eager anticipation on her face. She couldn't seem to shoo me out the door faster.

As soon as I hung up the phone with my mom who was checking on my flight and airport pick-up arrangements later today that was exactly what Wanda did.

She gave me a wink and a thumbs-up at the front door. "You're doing the right thing!" she called out.

That proclamation almost made me spin straight back inside and spill absolutely everything.

But with the guilt already gnawing inside me, I needed a

few quiet minutes to walk it off anyway so I could sort things out in my head.

I pulled my jacket closed closer to my neck. I still felt cold but I knew it wasn't the weather.

It was rationalizing time.

That was all totally fixable. Wanda still had no idea about us. All I needed to do was convince Lachlan to take her back.

Besides, I was about to go home in less than six hours. I was about to put all of this mess behind me.

I also decided right then that maybe I was giving up too soon on Jason.

Just like Wanda and Lachlan, Jason and I had history too. And it would be a shame to miss out on us after having waited all this time.

I was about to have my own happily ever after, and on New Year's Eve no less.

Meanwhile, Wanda and Lachlan would have all the time in the world to patch things up between them while I was gone.

"I'm doing the right thing," I mumbled to myself as I trudged down the tree-lined path, grimacing as I sidestepped slushy puddles again.

The sun had finally come out and the frosty tips of tree branches in the neighborhood gleamed as they began to melt.

Wanda had found out where Lachlan was staying and given me the address. The flat was nearby as he'd mentioned before, among a row of bungalows that must also serve as college housing.

I took a deep breath, rang the bell, and as soon as Lachlan's staunch face appeared at the door, a sudden urge to flee came over me but I willed myself to settle down.

I just had to do this one last thing and then I was going to catch my flight and everything would finally be over.

Lachlan stood by the open doorway. "What are you doing here?"

For a split second, I thought the coldness in his eyes wavered. He tipped his head to one side as if trying to measure my intentions.

When he moved to take a step closer, I blurted it out. "Wanda asked me to look for you."

He stopped short as though I had struck him, disappointment clear in his eyes that I hadn't come out here of my own volition.

I gestured behind me. "Could we take a walk?"

Lachlan glared at me and I thought he was going to slam the door in my face but he just moved to reach for his coat.

Any other day, it would have been lovely to be taking a walk down the snow-covered lane all the way to the frozen pond where a handful of couples and children decked out in mittens and wools were swooshing around on skates.

When I'd finally composed myself, I paused to meet Lachlan's gaze, affecting an air like this was nothing but a simple business transaction.

"Wanda says she wants you back," I relayed, matter-of-factly. "She says that the kiss with Doug was an accident and that it's definitely over between the two of them."

Lachlan's eyes darkened. "Are you doing this again? Are you in charge of making all of Wanda's excuses for her?"

I went for understanding. "Look, I know you're upset—"

He scoffed. "Upset? Upset doesn't half cover it. I can't even believe it took me this long to figure it out." He tilted his head in supposition. "Wanda would go out with that ape. Meanwhile, you were assigned to keep me busy." He shook his head. "And I was the moron who fell for it."

I wanted to argue but he wasn't finished.

"And the worst part is I don't even know why I'm not mad at you right now. I should be. I shouldn't want to see you ever again. I shouldn't still be hoping that maybe—" He stopped to blow out a breath. "That maybe without meaning to...you've also fallen for me."

The lump in my throat was making it difficult to swallow. "This is not about me right now," I reasoned. "This is about you and Wanda." I gave him a pointed look. "You should hear everything she's been saying about you. She says she's so proud of how far you've come and all that you've accomplished." I averted my gaze. "And she's so worried that because of all that, you wouldn't want her anymore."

Lachlan's forehead creased. "That's not why," he told me. "I'll admit I am grateful to her. But I realized that was all it was."

He shrugged in frustration. "I did want it to work out but she could never be bothered. I was the one who always had to be at her beck and call. And it just got to a point where it was getting harder and harder to remember why we were even together."

"That's why I just picked up, left, and came straight here. I didn't know exactly what I was looking for but I was finally sure I was ready to look."

"Then I found you and I realized something." He reeled his thoughts back from the recollection, cracking a small smile. "I had thought it was so hard with Wanda because I just wanted to be free. But I think...it was hard because I knew it wasn't real."

A momentary shadow of remorse was gone from his face as fast as it came. He turned to me, his gaze earnest. "This." He braced his hands on my arms before sliding them down to clasp both of mine in his. "This feels real. And I can't even believe how lucky I am."

I had to tamp down the surge of elation in my chest and I squeezed my eyes shut for a moment before finding the strength to pull away. "No. No. Don't."

He dropped his arms. "Ashleigh, we like each other. It's perfectly normal, perfectly okay. And frankly, I think it's perfect."

I met his gaze, those gorgeous, hopeful gray eyes, and swallowed hard again.

"Tell me," he implored. "There has to be something I can say, something I can do."

I didn't want to say 'no' one more time. I wavered in my stance.

What was I doing? Lachlan was the smartest, most generous, supportive, and understanding guy I had ever met.

Was I really going to let myself walk away from him? Was I going to settle for the ghost of Jason and our past relationship?

We know you deserve way more than you give yourself. Sometimes you have to take what you want.

But I knew what accepting Lachlan would mean. Was I prepared to risk my friendship with Wanda over a guy? Even if he turned out to be *the* guy?

I looked away in hesitation, in upset—which ended up

lucky because who else must be coming down the walkway around the pond toward us?

Gilbert Lawson, of course, his head cocked to one side, his gaze already on me—on us.

Maybe he'd overheard. Maybe he'd noticed Lachlan and I were having some kind of argument. Maybe he thought he was coming to my rescue.

I sucked my breath in, turning panicked eyes to Lachlan who had only to glance up to notice what had gotten me distracted and his eyes widened for a moment in understanding.

And when he met my gaze again, that same intensity flashed in his gray eyes, and also somehow, a firm resolution.

Without another word, Lachlan reached out for me and sealed my lips with his.

Red hot warmth flushed right through me and my eyes closed of their own accord.

Lachlan's eager fingers curled around the nape of my neck, digging into my hair, almost tugging on it as he closed his fist tight, tilting my head back.

He pressed against me, all heat and strength, backing me up to the fence and when I couldn't help a soft moan in his mouth, a groan rumbled in his chest.

Did the world stop spinning? It must have.

I had tumbled headlong into some kind of blissful, hazy heaven where all that mattered, all I knew, and all I could sense was Lachlan.

Lachlan and his worlds-ending, logic-defying, searing kiss.

I could barely hear anything else over the sound of my heart pounding in my ears.

Not even the highly audible haggard gasp of disbelief from

someone distinctly *not* Gilbert Lawson coming from a few feet away.

It seriously took a mighty effort to break away and turn to look.

But there stood Wanda in her faux fur parka and leather boots. Her eyes were red and wide, her mouth hanging open, face pale, fists balled up at her sides.

Oh, here we go.

16

Busted

Lachlan seemed less surprised than I was. He merely broke off and looked over as calm as anything.

Wanda's gaze flickered from me to Lachlan and back again, shaking her head, her eyes so big and green.

I bore her scrutiny, guilt all over my face.

Her expression changed from surprise to sheer disbelief to pure hatred, her eyes flashing in rage.

That's when Gilbert decided to interject. "Um...is everything okay?"

And Wanda's fury found a temporary target. "For the last time, Gilbert, stop stalking Ashleigh. It's weird and creepy and she hates you!"

I gasped, turning horrified eyes to Gilbert.

His jaw had dropped in shock but processing that statement along with his pre-existing fear of Wanda was a bit too much for him that he spun and fled.

"Wanda—!" I gestured toward the fleeing Gilbert in concern.

But Hurricane Wanda had made landfall.

She charged toward us, toward Lachlan, shoving him back in fury. "Is this you trying to get back at me?" she demanded. "And with my roommate? Ultimate low, man!" She pushed him again. "How could you even—?"

Lachlan tilted his head, regarding her with a look. "Well, I suppose I had a great teacher," he replied wryly.

Wanda shot him daggers before turning to glare at me. "Ashleigh, what the heck do you even think you're doing?"

I shook my head vigorously. "It's-It's not what you think. We were just pretending for Gilbert."

Wanda's jaw dropped in skepticism. "Oh, come off it. We both know you are not that good an actress."

Lachlan didn't like how Wanda was speaking to me. "Why don't you just leave her alone?"

Wanda scoffed again in incredulity as she turned her rage back to him. "Oh my gosh, are you actually defending her?" she asked, aghast. "What exactly is going on here?"

Lachlan pursed his lips. "Wanda, I've been trying to tell you all week but you seemed preoccupied dating dumb jocks." He went on without even flinching, "I want to break up."

Wanda's jaw dropped even lower. "What—because of her?" She pointed a disdainful finger at me.

He groaned. "No! Because of us!" He blew out an exasperated breath. "These past months we've barely been a couple. You already know you were never really happy with me. And me, I was just too scared to let you go," he admitted.

"Then when I'd finally built up enough courage to, you

wouldn't even see me. And Ashleigh just..." he trailed off, not really needing to elaborate.

Heaving, Wanda took a few steps back like she'd been punched in the gut, her narrowed eyes moving back and forth between Lachlan and myself again.

"Huh." She shook her head, mumbling in incredulity, "Well, that's just great, isn't it?" She whirled around to stalk away, her boots stamping hard on the snow.

"No, Wanda, wait—" I started after her but Lachlan caught my arm.

"Ashleigh—"

"Let me go." I tried to shrug him off. "Wanda's gone. Congratulations. You've gotten her back."

He blinked in offense. "Excuse me?"

I pulled away with all my strength. "That was just you trying to get back at Wanda!"

"What if it was? It still doesn't mean I didn't want to kiss you."

My head was spinning. I couldn't even rack my brain to come up with a plan to convince Wanda that—that—oh heck, she was absolutely right.

I groaned out a haggard sigh. "You could have at least let her down easy..."

"Oh, I'm sorry. I didn't know you were an expert on breaking up," he drawled.

Sick to my stomach, I dropped my gaze to the ground. "She's going to hate me."

"Maybe she should."

I blinked hard. What even was he talking about now? "Wanda's my friend!" I protested.

"That doesn't mean she owns you," Lachlan pointed out.

I shot him an incredulous glare. "What is that supposed to mean?"

He pursed his lips. "It means I know," he declared. "Ashleigh, I used to be you. I used to think all I needed to do was keep my head down, do what I'm told, accept whatever comes. And by trying to please everyone else, I forgot to work for what *I* wanted."

He gave me an even look. "But you have to live your own life, even if sometimes that means being selfish." He blew out a breath. "You can't hide in Wanda's shadow forever, Ashleigh."

That hit a nerve and I shot him an indignant look. "I'm not hiding."

His eyebrows rose. "Aren't you?"

I clenched my jaw. "And what about you? You've gone so far past the other side you've stopped considering other people's feelings, and believe me, nobody likes that guy."

He scoffed in ridicule. "Are you kidding me? Everyone likes me so much better now that—"

"Oh, what, now that you're a jerk and a complete phony? Flirting with all the girls and rationalizing all of your bad decisions. Oh, I see Wanda definitely was a good teacher." I shook my head, forging on. "I'm sorry but I don't want to end up like you, with you, near you—"

He winced like I'd struck him.

I was still heaving but I'd run out of words.

It seemed he had too.

Lachlan took a deep breath, his eyes cloudy with remorse. He took a step back then another.

Spent and achingly hollow, all I could do was watch him trudge backward, pivot on his heel, then walk away.

***

The day wasn't even over yet.

A rolled-up pair of socks flew past my head as soon as I came through our room door and I looked up in alert.

Wanda's face was still fuming red as she stood by her bed. She grabbed a crumpled-up tie-dyed T-shirt and pitched it at me before directly fetching two more tops to do the same thing.

A metal zipper grazed my cheek. "Ow!"

"Good! I hope that hurts," she cried out even as she reached for more items to chuck over, one of which was a ceramic figurine that when I managed to dodge to avoid it, smashed to pieces against the door.

"How—how could you even do this to me? You. How?" Her tone was in full disbelief like I had done something she never would have imagined I could in million years.

I heaved a huge sigh in exhaustion. "I didn't do this *to* you, Wanda," I corrected. "I didn't do anything to you."

"Who do you think you're kidding?" Wanda's eyes blazed. "I was there! I saw you with him!"

"Because I was trying to get you back together with him like you asked," I reminded her pointedly. "I was doing it *for* you."

"Oh, yeah, bravo." Wanda clapped her hands. "I'm sure you were making terrific progress especially at that last part when you kissed him!"

"Look, I know it was wrong—"

She scoffed. "Oh, you can bet your little—" Her next words muffled. "You were definitely wrong!"

As it happened, I was a little angry myself. "It just happened, okay? It's not like we planned to do that right in front of you."

"Oh, you must be so disappointed you got caught. Who knows what the heck you two have been doing behind my back these past few days?"

I blinked hard. "Are you serious right now? You have been out with Doug all week. How could you even be upset about this?"

"Because I thought you were my friend! I thought you could never do anything like this."

I threw up my hands in sudden understanding. "Oh right, so you wanted me to be more aggressive and stand up for myself, just not against you," I added with more sarcasm in my tone.

Wanda glared at me. "Do you even realize you are just a total rebound from me?" she mocked. "Poor sad, little Ashleigh. Always settling for my scraps."

I gritted my teeth, starting to heave. "Lachlan was going to break up with you!" I reminded her. "*That* was why he came. And do you even realize why?" I prompted in expectation.

Wanda folded her arms across her chest, averting her gaze like she didn't care but I couldn't hold back any longer.

"Because you *are* a selfish, self-centered hoe who didn't even appreciate the great guy you already had. You had to keep drooling over big, tough jocks just to make yourself feel better." I pointed my finger at her. "And I told you this would happen if you keep messing around."

"How many times have I even saved you this week, huh? Do you even realize I have been bailing you out of every stupid little thing you've happily traipsed into for years?"

"I don't even know why I've just been taking it. Maybe I *was* just in awe of you too. Or maybe I really was happy to hide in your shadow. Or maybe," I proposed emphatically. "I actually felt sorry for you. Because without poor, sad little Ashleigh, who else would put up with your crap?"

"Shut up!" Wanda shouted, flinging a set of headphones wildly, no longer even caring where she aimed. "Just shut up! You can have Lachlan. You can have any guy you want. You can just go home to your boring little life and get out of mine! And I'm sorry—no—I *hate* that I ever met you," she seethed before whirling around to go for a dramatic exit.

Except the door got caught on a pair of yoga pants on the floor and wouldn't slam shut.

Wanda let out a loud, frustrated groan. "This stupid door!"

I rolled my eyes. "Pick up your stupid yoga pants! Look at this mess!" I gestured to the rest of the room that now looked like a real hurricane had gone through it.

Wanda narrowed her eyes at me in fury. "This mess is just as much yours as it is mine, Ashleigh." She scoffed picking up the pants to toss them carelessly away before meeting my gaze again.

"And you can put your mind at ease," she reassured with a sneer. "I'll definitely be looking for other accommodation as soon as possible. With any luck, I'll be out of here before you even come back from snoozeville."

And with that, Wanda spun around, the door slamming shut behind her, punctuating her walk-out.

I blew out a sudden breath as the room fell silent and I cast a glance around the disaster area that was our room.

My chest ached and my throat was raw.

Well, at least Wanda got one thing right.

This was the best worst vacation ever.

17

Family

I almost missed my freaking flight.

But the warm air that accosted me coming out of the air-port terminal was like a comforting wave of relief.

So was the sight of our split-level suburban tract house as my dad drove the car onto the driveway, stopping just before the closed garage door.

I was a bit confused though as I peered through the sheer-curtained windows.

"Is the New Year's Eve party tonight?" I had to ask as Dad led the way and pushed the door open.

He cast me a wry sideways glance. He was well aware the party was tomorrow. "You'd think so, wouldn't you?" He heaved my suitcase down off his shoulder and set it on the floor by the shoe rack before yelling out, "Celia, we're back!"

Noisy chatter, laughter, clinking glasses, and the smell of

cinnamon and fresh baking greeted me as I ventured down the hallway.

Our living room was exactly the picture they had sent me. Teddy bears, green wreaths, and red bows everywhere. Twinkling lights hung from the mantel and every other nook and cranny imaginable.

What was not in the picture was the half dozen of my relatives who were lounging around on the couch or walking through the archway between the dining room and the kitchen, holding glasses of drinks and what looked like canapes.

My nana, sitting in the big comfy armchair noticed me first. "Ashleigh," she greeted with a crinkly smile, waving me over.

"Hi, Nana! Merry Christmas." I returned her smile as I approached, already bending down to kiss her cheek.

She grasped my arms, giving me a top-to-toe once-over. "My, you're putting on some weight, my dear."

My smile froze on my face, not exactly in disbelief, but more like 'Ah, yes, of course.'

"Thanks, Nana." I bit back my grin as I moved away, casting an absent glance over at my grandpa dozing on one end of the couch before coming through the archway toward the kitchen where my mom and a couple of my aunts were congregated.

"Well, sure. But they'll just do it wrong anyway and I'd have to redo the whole—" Mom looked up distracted upon spotting me. "Ashleigh, you're home!"

"Hi, Mom—"

She walked past the kitchen island for a big bear hug. "We

missed you at Christmas, sweetie. All your gifts are still under the tree. And look, everyone's here."

"I noticed."

"Oh, your aunts were just in the neighborhood anyway," she explained directly pulling away to gesture to one of them. "Your Aunt Angie was just talking about her son, your cousin Blythe. Do you know he's just passed the bar exam? He'll be sitting in the supreme court soon." Her tone had a tinge of envy in it as he was not *her* son.

Aunt Angie waved it away self-effacingly before turning to my Aunt Beth. "Did you add something new to these macaroons, Beth? They are absolutely divine," she crooned.

"I'm using coconut sugar now," Aunt Beth replied with a gleam in her eye.

Aunt Angie was nodding. "I see, I see." She took another bite. "They're almost as good as *my* macaroon recipe."

"Oh."

"Jim!" My mom's face was wrinkled in distaste as she leaned back, peering at something in the hallway. "Why is Ashleigh's suitcase in the foyer?"

"I don't know!" came the equally yelled-out reply from somewhere in the house.

"Mom," I started.

Mom groaned in exasperation. "What am I going to do about your father, Ashleigh? Why didn't he just take your bag straight upstairs instead of leaving it there a mess?"

"It's okay, Mom. I can do it."

"Honestly, it's common sense. I don't understand how things like this don't just occur naturally to him. They're plain as day to me. I sincerely hope you don't take after that side of the family."

"Is Dad hiding in the TV room again?" I had to ask.

"I don't know. Your Uncle Jude is watching 'Dancing with the Stars'," she relayed offhand.

"Is Stacy at home with the baby right now?" Aunt Angie asked Aunt Beth who nodded.

"Yes! They took that sleep training class that Twinkie recommended and it's done wonders for little Archie."

"Oh, we don't believe in sleep training. We co-slept Blythe and he's turned out into a very fine young man."

I stifled my disparaging chuckle as I reached for a macaroon.

One of my aunts turned to me. "What do you take in school again, dear?"

"Biochemistry medicine," I replied.

"Oh, of course, just like your mom." My aunt smiled.

"Well, not exactly," my mom corrected as she rearranged some plates on the counter. "Ashleigh's actually thinking to go more into research instead of practical pharmacology." She gave me a look and a short nod. "But we think it's still a really promising field, don't we?"

I plastered another smile on my face, resisting the urge to stuff seventeen macaroons in my mouth all at once.

For a moment there, I had forgotten all about what had been going on with me this past week.

Yes. I was home.

Dad was in the garage, tinkering with his ham radio collection. I stepped over a box of old Christmas lights as I walked over.

"So this is where you're hiding nowadays."

Dad had a sly grin, his screwdriver poised in the air. "Your mom's siblings are inside. Where else do you think I would be?"

I chuckled as I came up to the workbench. "I don't understand. Don't they all hate each other?" I mused in confusion, absently rifling through a box of rusty old dials.

He turned his attention back to the radio. "It resets every Christmas. Haven't you noticed? They take a break from their all-year hatred to eat food and exchange lousy presents."

That made me laugh. "So I gather the silk scarf didn't make an impression?" I prompted as he and I had quite some trouble selecting a Christmas gift for my super picky mother —as we did every year.

He gave me an even glance. "When have you ever heard your mom appreciate any gift she's been given? There's always something wrong with it."

I let out a helpless sigh, slumping down onto one of the bar stools. "Dad, why is nothing ever good enough for Mom?"

Dad didn't even look over as he replied, "Your mom just has a different set of standards. She always has."

Gloomy, I picked at the broken bits on the table, and Dad gave me a sideways narrowed gaze.

"Something wrong, Ash?"

I pursed my lips. "I just...I feel like I can't ever do anything right with her. And whatever I do, no matter how hard I try, it's like I still keep hearing her voice in my head. '*Why isn't it better? It could always be better. You're going to do it wrong. Don't even think about it.'"*

Dad put his tools down, his forehead creased as he turned to me. "Sweetie, I'm sure your mother doesn't think that. And whatever else your mother likes to complain about—" He paused, giving me a meaningful glance as Mom was wont to do that *a lot.* "It doesn't mean she doesn't love you." He puffed up his chest. "Besides, there's nothing wrong with making mistakes. I make them every day."

"Mom doesn't." I shook my head. "I wish I didn't," I mumbled, definitely referring to particularly sore, particularly recent events.

Dad laughed, reaching out to ruffle my hair in reassurance. "Yes, she does. In any case, I don't want you to be too worked up trying to be exactly like Mom. Especially since you already know it won't ever be good enough anyway," he quipped wryly.

He shrugged before he turned back to his radios. "Just try your best to be exactly like *you.*" He motioned with his screwdriver. "Write that down. That's some good advice from your not-at-all-perfect dear old dad."

And my shoulders shook in mirth.

18

Decisions

"Did you set the timer on the oven? The roast should finish just before the guests arrive so the meat can rest."

I nodded as I unloaded the measuring cups and spoons I was struggling to hold onto into the sink for washing before turning to set the oven timer.

Mom was bustling between the kitchen island and the stove, checking on pots and pans of even more food.

In case it wasn't obvious yet, Christmas was always a busy time in our house.

This morning, I'd had to sit through my mother's annual sorting through Christmas gifts to determine which ones were good enough to re-gift before spending the next hour wrapping about a dozen last-minute gifts for relatives we hadn't been expecting would be flying in for the party tonight.

Since then I'd had to help my mom with food preparations,

table setup, a bit of redecorating, and icing like a billion Christmas cookies.

Apparently, my dad simply could not be relied on to assist her with any of these tasks. He had been sent away on the easiest of errands to buy ice—with any luck, the right kind.

I supposed I should have been pleased that at least my mom still thought I could be trusted to do certain things up to par.

"Oh also don't forget to put some music on," Mom piped up from her station at the stove.

"Okay." I nodded again and settled down at the counter with the assortment of remote controls to set up the multimedia system.

In between basting and tasting, Mom glanced up to give me a prompting smile. "I almost forgot to ask. How's Wanda, dear? Is she still at the boarding house?"

And my stomach dropped to my toes.

"Oh." I tried to resist the urge to grimace. "Yeah, she didn't go home again. She's fine, I guess."

"She seems like such a nice girl. I feel sorry for her what with her parents' situation and all."

That note hitting home, I took a deep disheartened breath. "Well actually...Wanda and I kind of had a fight."

Mom didn't divert her attention from the pasta sauce. "Really? Do you want to talk about it?"

I narrowed my eyes, not sure if I did.

I'd already gone through the agonizing replay of events multiple times in my head and now far removed from the situation, I'd identified the plethora of missteps and mistakes involved from both sides—Wanda's and mine.

And aside from my concern that the pasta sauce might burn, I wasn't really eager to rehash the whole thing.

Last week, I would have automatically responded in understanding, said that I was probably the one who was wrong anyway and formulated some sort of rationalization as to why.

Today, there was an uneasy feeling in my gut as I considered how much I'd actually let Wanda take over my life.

Yes, I made excuses for Wanda. But really I'd been using her as an excuse as well. Because as long as she made all the decisions, there was hardly any chance that I would make the wrong ones.

Poor, sad Ashleigh. Can't grow a backbone. Can't even make her own decisions.

But Mom didn't press on. Instead, she turned to retrieve a teaspoon from the drawer so she could taste the sauce.

I supposed there were more important things to do than to dwell on my likely petty, personal problems.

Deep in thought, I stared at the roast sizzling in the oven.

Ding!

I blinked as an egg timer went off, as though of an epiphany sparking in my head.

"Time to check the meat," Mom spoke up, and distracted, I moved to let her pass.

What was that thing people said about the New Year? Everybody gets a fresh start?

I was so tired of holding myself back.

Think about how much stress you're putting yourself under... You'd just feel so relieved to be able to be yourself...

Maybe it was finally time to ask for what I wanted for

a change. Even if it ended up in a confrontation. Even if it turned out to be a complete mistake.

I hesitated before looking up at my mom again. I could just imagine the chaos once all my relatives arrived for tonight's party. There was no better time to bring this up.

"Hey, Mom…do you remember that I've always been good with computers?"

"Mm-hmm," she replied, peering into a saucepot.

I swallowed hard, trying to hold it together. "Well, what do you think if…" My heart started pounding in my chest. I could already see her disappointed looks, hear her displeased criticism. I thought I was going to throw up.

Stay strong. You can do this.

I took another deep breath. "Um, I was thinking that I…might actually take up some Computer Science courses at school this semester. It's a really exciting and diverse field of study with a very stable job market," I rushed on to relay.

"Oh." Mom paused for thought. "That's interesting, honey. But I thought you wanted to be in science research, like Dad and I?"

"Well, yes, but I think I could also enjoy multimedia or software design. I think I might be really good at it too." I wrinkled my nose, already dreading her response. "Would you mind?"

Her eyebrows rose. "Mind? Why would we mind? Honey, this is your education," she told me. "I think you're an adult now and you're fully capable of making decisions yourself."

My eyes widened. "Really?"

"Of course." She shrugged as if I should have already known that.

My stomach churned. I supposed I was even more than a little uncertain in my decision-making skills of late, especially if I were to judge based on recent events.

I chewed on my bottom lip. "But what if I make the wrong decisions or choose the wrong thing?"

Mom was focused on whisking her ganache, speaking slowly. "You know the thing about decisions dear is that…most of the time they're not really right or wrong. You just…make your choices as best you can and then you deal with the consequences."

I stilled for a moment as her advice seemed to permeate through every layer of apprehension and baggage I'd been holding on to for so long.

I broke a smile, a heavy burden lifting from my chest.

Sure, my mother drove me crazy but she was still the smartest woman I knew.

"You're the only one who can really plan your life," Mom went on assuredly. "You have to choose your own future, your own career, your own job."

Then she picked up a wooden spoon to wave in the air to amend, "But you know, something respectable. Something in an office.

That addendum made me laugh. "Thanks, Mom."

***

My cousins tore through the living room, bumping past me to run upstairs, a direction from which I could hear my youngest cousin Archie who was only eight months old bawling out.

A group of older kids was gathered around the TV where someone had set up a gaming console.

Grandparents were arranged strategically around the lounge suite, aunts were crowding the kitchen to collect their empty platters post-dinner, and my Uncle Jude was walking around training his camera on literally anything as he bellowed out.

"Smile!"

Blinking the spots from my eyes, I walked over to the buffet table where Mom had decked out the desserts and I swiped a couple of marshmallows off a pie before moving back through the living room again, dodging another wayward nephew scooting underfoot.

I could imagine the scenes had been the same at last week's Christmas party—when I should have been here instead of being stuck at the dorms with Wanda and having the worst week of my life.

If only I had been able to go home back then, I wouldn't have gotten between Wanda and Lachlan at all, and both of them would still be speaking to me right now.

Though it was probably for the better.

I needed to be able to navigate my own life without relying on Wanda or anyone else to lead. I had to start taking responsibility for my own decisions which meant I had to start making them—by myself, and not just going along with whoever had the loudest voice.

And Lachlan, well...I should have known that was a non-starter from Day 1.

Wanda had been totally on-point about him. He had been

conflicted, vulnerable, and obviously just on a total rebound, and I happened to be the most convenient target.

Even if...

I stopped that thought, shaking my head briskly.

Total rebound. Period.

In any case, I figured it certainly couldn't get any worse than this.

When the doorbell rang, everyone else was occupied so I hurried to get it and my greeting died on my lips as I swung the door open.

His blue eyes lit up as they met mine. "Ashleigh!"

I almost had to snap myself back to the present. I'd gotten so used to only seeing him in pictures for the last few years that I almost couldn't believe I was really seeing him.

My jaw dropped in delight. "Jason! Oh my gosh, you're finally here." I threw my arms around his neck.

He chuckled as he hugged me back. "Happy New Year, Ash. It's been a minute."

It was the rush of seeing an old friend, the rush of fond old memories and happy times shared.

Yes, I was thrilled to see him again. But while it felt familiar and warm to finally be together again, what I felt most was, ironically, distance.

Jason pulled away to smile at me before he thrust a shiny gift-wrapped package toward me, asking, "How could you miss Christmas?"

But I returned his smile, not dispirited at all. "You don't even want to know."

After taking Jason to say hello to my folks, stealing a couple of slices of pie while skillfully managing to avoid being force-fed leftover peas and cornbread, the two of us raced to the backyard, still laughing as he recounted a similar Christmas six years ago.

We sat down on the porch steps with our plates of food.

"I still can't believe you're finally back in California." I nudged his knee. "Aren't you boiling in this tropical weather?"

"Haha," he mocked. "You know I'd still rather be too hot than too cold."

"So how's your mom and dad?"

"Good." He nodded as he relayed, "I think my dad is thinking of finally retiring and he and Mom want to stay here."

"That's great!" I gushed.

"In fact, I'm finishing my degree early so I can basically do what I want now," he remarked with a grin.

I nodded, as impressed as he looked elated. "You can even visit me at school," I suggested. "You know, I finally talked my mom into letting me take some computer courses. Remember? I've always had a knack for it so I thought, why not?"

His forehead creased as he took a bite of his pie. "Really? But you're a junior. That's a lot of extra, unnecessary work to be putting on to your academic load this late."

I furrowed my eyebrows a little. I was hoping he would be as excited as I was. But then I dismissed it as obviously, he wouldn't have had any idea the struggle I'd gone through to even have that conversation.

"Oh. Well. I mean, I can work harder. And there's no harm in trying, right?" I proposed, carefully carving out a bite of my dessert with a fork.

He shrugged noncommittally. "I suppose."

I chewed on my mouthful but instantly wrinkled my nose as a certain tangy taste rolled on my tongue.

Jason noticed my pause. "What's wrong?"

"Oh, I got the dumb key lime pie instead of the banana cream." I rolled my eyes, laughing. "It was really hard to pay attention when I was trying to dodge my aunts."

"Oh." He nodded and turned back to his own plate. "That's fine. It's not like you can't eat it."

An odd chuckle escaped my throat. "Right."

After swallowing his mouthful, Jason elbowed me. "Hey, don't forget to open your present."

My eyes lit up again and I set my plate down to reach for the box beside me, tugging on the ribbon and easily lifting the lid to peek inside.

I blinked at the contents of the box. "Aviators and a map of North Dakota...?"

"Yeah, remember? We went to that air show once and you said you loved it," Jason recalled. "And I thought the two of us could do a road trip this spring break. There's a pilot school in North Dakota and my dad and I were talking about me going to the academy in the fall."

"Oh. Right." I examined the sunglasses closely with the porch light reflecting on them.

Except I didn't have the faintest recollection of having gone to any air show or even what he was talking about.

"I've planned out the trip already," he relayed, polishing off the last of his pie. "You just need to come back to L.A. in March. We can rent a car just like we always said."

I tried to think ahead to March. "I'm not sure what I've got planned for spring break yet."

He put his hand up. "No, no. You cancel those. You won't want to miss this trip of a lifetime. It sounds great, right?"

"Oh. Yeah, that sounds..." I was already nodding when I caught myself, that voice already nagging in the back of my head.

Something about how you shouldn't simply keep settling for what you're offered...

"Actually." I straightened up to give Jason an even look. "No. I can't."

"Beg your pardon?"

I blinked, taking a deep breath. "No, Jason. It's really sweet and it sounds...interesting but I'm not really that into flying."

"What? Of course, you are. We both love it. You told me that time."

"Well," I amended. "I might have. I mean I do like airplanes but not as much as you. Not enough to do all that. Honestly, I don't even remember."

"Really?" He quirked his head in puzzlement.

I grimaced. "Sort of. Yeah."

His mouth had dropped open. "Wow."

"I'm sorry if this is out of nowhere." I fidgeted in my seat. "There's a lot of things I'm only just realizing lately."

"But I've already planned everything. And if you don't do this with me, we might not see each other again for a while. A *long* while." His eyes widened in the calculation.

"Yeah." It took me a moment to register that I wasn't half as disappointed as I thought I would be.

Jason and I had been apart longer than we'd been together. And for the first time, I could imagine a day when I didn't pine away for him or wait for his call.

His eyebrows furrowed as he studied my expression, almost as though he was already reading my mind. "So actually...when you said 'no', you really meant 'goodbye'..."

I tilted my head, giving him a consoling look after a moment. "I can call you," I offered with a shrug. "We're good with distance."

I could see the displeasure bubbling up his chest and I was bracing myself to hear it out loud when—

"Ash! Jason!" someone yelled from inside and I jumped in surprise.

My mom poked her head out of the door. "Come on, you two," she beckoned. "They're starting the countdown."

I met Jason's troubled gaze for a moment before glancing up to force a smile at Mom in response. "Okay, we'll be right in."

Mom grinned, a sort of scheming look on her face as she misunderstood the situation. "You kids," she teased before heading back inside and closing the door.

When I turned to him again, Jason was staring at the grass, his blue eyes deep in thought, his blonde hair glimmering underneath the outdoor fairy lights strung across the porch overhang.

My heart was pounding in my chest again, but this time in melancholy.

I did like Jason—a previous version of him. Back when I was a previous version of me. And I would always cherish those memories with him but that was all they were now. Memories.

I had been certain that if it ever came to this, I was

resolved to let him down easy. But maybe there really was no simple way to break up with someone.

Someone always ended up hurt.

My shoulders sagged as I watched Jason's form retreat through the darkened garden and unlatch the lane gate.

"5...4...3..."

The countdown resounded from inside.

"2...1... *Happy New Year!*"

The sky lit up with all kinds of whorls and colors of fireworks, the night air filling with noise, cheers, and shouts of joy.

Sighing, I stared at the half-eaten plate of key lime pie on the wooden step beside me.

19

Sorry

"Thank you." I gave the clerk a small smile as I walked away from the registration table.

It was the first day back at school after the decidedly too short New Year break I'd spent at home trying to forget that I sucked at making decisions.

Nonetheless, I had decided to bite the bullet and actually apply for those Computer Science courses.

I figured there was no harm in trying it out and that if I worked my butt off and it panned out, I might even end up with a double major diploma.

That would definitely make my parents happy.

But more to the point, it would make *me* happy.

Stella was waiting for me by the quad. She'd found me the moment I'd arrived and wouldn't relent until I paid up on that outstanding IOU. Suffice it to say, she was now fully caught up on recent events.

She eyed the suitcase I was lugging around as I approached her. "So you really haven't been back to the boarding house yet?"

I gave her a look. "What do you think?"

I was dreading seeing Wanda.

I was also dreading seeing her half of the room potentially gone.

Admittedly, I had cooled off quite a bit since New Year's and I was sure I wanted to make up with her. I just wasn't sure how.

"Did you see her over the break?"

Stella shrugged as we walked down the lane, dodging the streams of students hurrying to places. "Just once at The Corner. I think she figured we all probably already knew about what had happened because she was just as eager to avoid us as we were to avoid her."

I frowned, almost in concern. "I hope she's okay."

"Well, if you ask me—," she began, her tone haughty.

"Oh, here we go."

Stella put a hand up. "You totally did the right thing. Wanda was being a prima diva and she got exactly what she deserved. If I were you, I'd avoid her right up to graduation," she advised firmly. Then after a pause, she rolled her shoulders, averting her gaze. "I'm only sorry she drove Lachlan away."

I shot her a warning glare. "Don't."

Admittedly, I wasn't prepared to deal with the Lachlan side of the equation just yet. Whenever my thoughts strayed to the few days we'd spent together, things that I had clear in my head turned fuzzy all over again.

And I'd already told Stella this.

"I'm just saying," Stella reasoned, matter-of-factly. "It looked like he made you happy." She returned my pointed glare. "That's all I want, Ash. I want you to be happy."

I noted her fierce, unfaltering expression and couldn't help a chuckle. Stella was my oldest and dearest friend. And I had recently witnessed what underappreciation did to a relationship.

I beamed a grateful smile, slinging my arm around her shoulders. "Thanks, Stella."

She pushed me away, feigning offense. "Dude, I have a boyfriend."

But I caught the impish glint in her eye and we both burst out laughing.

By noon, I decided there was no way I was going to drag my luggage with me around campus all day. I was still dreading it but I knew I was going to have to face Wanda eventually so I began my grim trudge toward the boarding house.

Turning the corner, I almost jumped when I spotted Gilbert walking down the lane toward me.

He saw me right away, his eyes widening briefly before he spun to escape.

"Gilbert, wait!" I called out as I ran up to block his path, luggage and all.

"Uh, hey, Ashleigh," he mumbled. I could see he was still trying to think of how to run past me.

I put my hand up. "Please, I want to apologize for what happened."

He shifted on his feet, not meeting my gaze. "Um, you know what, don't worry about it."

I shook my head. "Look, I don't want to make any more excuses for Wanda but I want to apologize for my part of it. I'm really sorry it had to come to that."

"It wouldn't have been the first time I was rejected by a pretty girl. You could have just told me," he kept mumbling.

"I know. I know that. Now." I nodded with a grimace. "I guess I was just trying to avoid hurting your feelings. Except it seems I ended up hurting them even more."

"Well, you know, I'll get over it. Eventually." He moved to shrug.

I reached out to pat his shoulder in consolation but to my surprise, he jerked away.

His gaze flitted up to meet mine for a split second. "I don't want your boyfriend to beat me up."

"Oh." I almost scoffed. "He wasn't my boyfriend."

Gilbert's eyebrows rose, huffing in skepticism. "He wasn't?" He kicked the slush on the ground before pivoting on his heel to walk away, but not without one last prying, offhand remark. "Then that must have been one heck of a friendly kiss."

A sudden warmth surged through me as a vivid recollection of that world-stopping kiss came right back for the first time after vacation, despite all that effort of trying to avoid thinking about it.

I froze in my tracks with the memory as freshly intense as though it had only happened yesterday...

Oh, for goodness sake—not now!

I had to shake my entire body briskly to banish the

electrifying sensation before turning to be on my way, reiterating that same mantra in my head.

Total rebound. Period.

The last thing I needed right now was to pine away for another new guy that I couldn't have.

Upon arriving up the stairs at the boarding house, I was surprised our room door was already open. I was also a bit surprised to see that everything was still a horrendous, enormous mess. Practically nothing had even been moved since I'd left for New Year's.

The same Christmas decorations, now-deflated balloons, candy wrappers, books, and shoes littered the room. The pile of laundry on both our beds had just grown as if it had developed self-replicating capabilities.

I shook my head, bending down to pick up pieces of the broken ceramic trinket to begrudgingly put in the trash can.

On my way to the corner, I fished out a pair of flip-flops from under the bed, only to find one dust-bunny-shaped leather boot under there too and I went to put that away as well.

As soon as I started cleaning up, I kept going.

I picked out empty potato chips bags and chocolate wrappers tangled within the bedsheets and pulled out stockings and random socks from under the mattress.

I almost didn't hear Wanda come into the room but the cold chill from her eyes was downright arctic when I met her gaze.

She didn't say anything but she headed over to her side, picking up one of the flip-flops I had dropped on the way.

I winced. "Sorry."

She narrowed her eyes at me but didn't respond.

Without a word, she tossed the flip-flop onto the shoe rack and began to arrange the disarray of shoes upon it, picking up an old hairbrush and a torn and wrinkled movie poster that had fallen behind it.

I pulled out a few of Wanda's skirts from under my pile of clothes and tossed them onto her bed.

At the same time, several pieces of clothing landed on my bed from Wanda's side.

I unearthed a stained pair of pants from inside a sweater, pausing as I held it up.

It was from that one time before a concert that for some reason, I was convinced I could jump over this mud puddle in the football field and ended up knee-deep in tar and mud.

Wanda had to help me wash my pants in the ladies' before attending the concert because of course, we couldn't miss that.

I couldn't help a smirk.

On the floor behind my table, I found Wanda's seashell frame of a photo of her and me from when the university did a Roaring Twenties bash and we both had too much peach schnapps.

I couldn't help a small chuckle at the recall. After the party, we had been so tipsy we could barely climb the stairs up the boarding house.

I turned to hand the frame to Wanda so she could put it away with her stuff.

Wanda's eyes softened as her gaze fell on it and I guessed the same memory had just recalled on her too. But she didn't say anything. She just kept on tidying up.

I hardly noticed when the sun began to dip low in the sky. We had been cleaning the room all afternoon.

When I looked around again, I could actually see the wooden floor. There was space to walk without worrying about pricking your feet or possibly tetanus.

The windowsills had been cleared of three semesters worth of styrofoam coffee cups. Clothes were folded and neatly piled at the foot of our beds and the closet door wasn't bursting full of haphazardly put-away dresses.

I took a deep, cleansing breath, unable to help a pleased smile at our surroundings.

My gaze fell on another framed photo hanging askew on the wall. It was of Wanda and me at the first orientation. She was trying to get me to smile bigger and I was trying to push her away.

I had thought she was the flakiest person I had ever met. She'd thought I was the most boring.

I couldn't even remember how we managed to get along at all at the beginning. But somehow we did. Maybe when they said opposites attract, they didn't just mean for couples but friends too.

And whatever else she was, Wanda was still my friend.

Last semester, when I was so sleep-deprived from doing a research paper, she always made sure we had snacks in the room so I wouldn't forget to eat.

She never forgot an occasion and would insist on making a big deal of birthdays and small achievements. She made the lamest things seem fun and always made sure we *carpe*'d the heck out of every *diem*.

I cast another glance around with a wistful sigh. It was

crazy how many memories were contained in this room alone. My heart squeezed when I thought of the things Wanda and I would never get to do again.

I stilled for a moment, steeling myself. I had to make this right. I had to fix things with Wanda.

Determined, I turned around, ready to fight for our friendship. "Wanda, I—"

But Wanda was sitting cross-legged on her bed, already crying.

I was taken aback. "What's wrong?"

Then I noticed what she had in her hand. It was a pamphlet for a social club that Wanda desperately wanted to join last year. And when she didn't make the cut and cried all day, I'd cut my classes just so I could stay with her all morning.

Wanda looked back up at me. "Oh, Ash, I'm so sorry. You were right. I've been taking everyone for granted."

I couldn't help another giant sigh of relief as I moved to sit down and hug her. "Oh my gosh, I'm sorry too. You have to know, I never meant to hurt you. I would never hurt you on purpose."

Wanda sniffled by my ear. "I was thinking how great a friend you are and I didn't want to lose you."

"You know what? I was thinking exactly the same thing." I pulled away with a rueful smile. "I shouldn't have said all those things last year. And I shouldn't have interfered—"

"Are you kidding?" she gawked. "If I am your bodyguard then you are my conscience. Please. Always tell me when I'm being a big dumb hoe." Then she paused to wrinkle her nose. "I mean I'll probably listen to you like ninety percent of the time—maybe eighty, seventy-five percent."

My amused chuckle was trapped in my throat when Wanda changed the subject.

"And about Locky..." she began, her tone decisive. "I know you were right. I wasn't being fair to him."

My smile faded at the melancholy look on her face despite her tone. But I was relieved she was able to bring up such a sensitive topic without even a hint of bitterness.

"I was thinking about it all week and...I think I never actually really saw him as a boyfriend, but more like—a project," she considered, her head tilted to one side.

I pursed my lips. It was no wonder Lachlan felt a bit trapped. But at least with her help, he'd also found the strength to realize it and move on. And vice versa.

Wanda nudged my shoulder. "It's stupid to fight over one stupid guy, right?" she ventured. "Even if he is a really good kisser."

That made me laugh and nod as I happened to agree on both counts. And if she and I could get past something like this then there might still be hope for our friendship.

She sniffled again, reaching for a tissue. "So did you see Locky over New Year's?"

I gave her a flat look to reiterate. "Come on. We both know he was just getting back at you for dating Doug. None of that stuff was real. You said it yourself. I was just a total rebound."

Wanda wrinkled her nose, a bit sheepish. "Oh, I don't know. Locky's not really a rebound kind of guy." A corner of her mouth turned up in recollection. "And I'd always thought you two had so much in common."

I had to concur, offhand, "We did."

"He was so much like you—smart, generous, always willing to see the best in others."

"He was."

"That's probably why I liked you both. It makes sense now that you would fall for each other."

I furrowed my eyebrows. Hearing Wanda say it out loud herself dropped a brand new heavy burden on my chest.

That maybe without meaning to...you've also fallen for me. And frankly, I think it's perfect.

"That's right..." I trailed off at the staggering realization. And after a long moment, I hung my head, shaking it in lament.

Or it *would* have been perfect.

I took a deep breath to collect myself. "That's really too bad then."

Wanda was watching my face. "Oh, Ash..."

"Yeah, well." I shrugged before letting out a small sigh. "And I officially broke up with Jason too. So I guess some things are just meant to stay in the past."

Wanda frowned in commiseration. But after a moment, her eyes lit up again in an entirely familiar manner. "Hey, do you know what this means?"

I was stunned speechless by her instant mood swap. Then again I supposed I shouldn't have been surprised anymore.

Wanda wiggled her eyebrows, a mischievous glint in her eyes. "Two of the school's hottest babes are single again. Mark my words. This year will be the absolute best ever!"

***

20

More Crepes

Spring break

Wifi. Crepes.

I stared at the chalk scrawled on the signboard outside the red brick building of a little downtown French café.

Perfect.

I stepped through the door and was greeted by the delicious aroma of assorted baked goods. I browsed the selection behind the counter with a smile, grateful that many establishments offered free internet with their coffees.

I hadn't even been home for a week yet and my mother was already driving me up the wall. She had decided that this week was the best time to spring clean our entire house and expecting help from my dad and me.

I already knew that was a recipe for a total disaster.

And with the past few months of school being grueling

178

and full-on with my additional new courses and having this massive paper to finish, I'd had to escape the house again today—laptop in tow, in the hopes of getting some work done.

But even though the decadence of the freshly baked danishes was incredibly tempting, I already knew what I wanted to order.

Because I hadn't stopped thinking about it since after New Year's. And him.

Lachlan.

I love hearing you say my name...

I held on to the memory of his voice, that still-diffident smile he got whenever he received compliments, the way those intense gray eyes always challenged me, encouraged me, reassured me...

I must have been spaced out for a while that the guy in the white hat behind the counter snapped his fingers in my face.

"Hey. I said are you going to order or not?"

I blinked, snapping to attention. "Oh. Right. Sure. Yes." I scanned the crepes menu behind his head and rattled off, "Could I please have the—la *burgery*...?" I grimaced in uncertainty.

"La Bergère," he corrected, not even looking up as he punched it in. No doubt, he was used to people mispronouncing the menu items.

"Great. Thanks."

I took my plastic number to one of the outdoor tables and promptly set up my laptop once I was seated.

Perhaps it was just as well that I had been buried in school work since New Year's. Daydreaming surely didn't take up too much time, compared to, say, scheming about how to get back in touch with him.

Even just to apologize. Never mind anything else.

Except I had no idea how to contact him. The number Wanda had had was for his friend's lodging back in Cambridge. I didn't know where he lived in L.A. or if he was boarding near the school.

And short of showing up at USC and stalking all the robotics courses, the only other thing I could think of was this.

Ironically, I was back to where I had been this time last year—pining away for some guy from afar. I was starting to think that maybe that was all I was good for.

Fidgeting in my seat, I narrowed my eyes as a happy couple walked past, hand in hand, airy laughter, whispering in each other's ear, striding down the sidewalk before veering off to cross the street. They were followed by a group of rowdy, noisy high-schoolers.

I was stopping to consider that maybe I should have gotten a table inside the café but then the crowds parted and I was looking at a familiar face.

I blinked, stunned.

Oh, for goodness sake, how on Earth could he possibly look even hotter than before?

With the warmer weather only necessitating the jeans and a T-shirt, I understood why he should indeed be offended at being called a 'bean pole.'

Lachlan had stopped in his tracks, having recognized me too, looking winded, and I thought something flickered in his eyes.

But after a second, he looked away, directly turning to head into the café.

My heart already in my throat, I swiveled in my chair, snapping my laptop shut, to watch through the glass as he came up to the counter to order.

I admit I had come here on the off chance that he was still in search of that elusive crepe that I might run into him but it was such a long shot I hadn't planned ahead as to what to do if he actually showed up.

Lachlan took his order number and ambled back outside.

I straightened up in my seat, beginning to heave in almost eager anticipation but he walked past me to take instead the table right behind mine, sitting with his back to me.

Dispirited, I sank back in my chair.

Lachlan shifted in his seat. I could almost glimpse his reflection in the window.

With a sour taste in my mouth, I wondered if he was meeting a date here. But before I could dwell on that, the waitress came by with my order and plunked it on the table before she moved to deliver a cup of coffee to him.

"Thanks."

I quirked my eyebrows as Lachlan's tone had been even and he hadn't made use of her name or made her giggle or anything.

But I dismissed that puzzlement as I waved the waitress back first. "Oh, excuse me." I gave her a hesitant smile. "Could I please get some extra honey? Thanks."

For those keeping score, I had gotten a lot better at talking to servers. I still didn't love it whenever I'd had to ask them something or send my food back but at least it was a start.

I examined my plate. Luckily, they had gotten the order correct today. In fact, the crepes looked absolutely mouth-watering except I seemed to have lost my appetite.

Lachlan's spoon clinked around his coffee cup and my chest constricted. A nagging voice in my head was telling me to finish eating quickly and run away.

I supposed it would have been easy to forget about him. Really, we had only spent roughly four days together over Christmas. But as far as decisions went, I was pretty sure this was one I'd regret if I let my cowardice get the better of me.

Stay strong. You can do this. Sometimes you have to take what you want, Ashleigh.

"I miss you." The words left my mouth before I could stop them.

I couldn't turn around, couldn't see his reaction, but after a few more nerve-wracking minutes of non-response with my heart pounding in my ears, I figured I might as well keep going.

I pushed my chair back with a loud screech, got up, and leaving all my stuff behind, slid into the seat across from Lachlan at his table.

His eyebrows had shot up in surprise but he didn't say anything.

I met his gaze evenly. "I need to apologize," I began with another business-like tone. "Look, you were right about me. I let Wanda get her way all the time and always put what I wanted aside. I've been terrified of making decisions and mistakes and because of that I've been making even more terrible decisions and mistakes."

Not responding or saying anything, Lachlan simply sat

back with a blank expression, observing my every movement, studying my face, my eyes.

"I'm taking Computer Science courses now. And Jason is definitely history—" I broke off as the bells above the café door jangled with the waitress coming out with my squeezy bottle of honey.

She paused in mid-stride to give me a confused look but went to bring my plate to me from the other table anyway before turning to leave again.

Lachlan's attention had turned to my plate and his eyes narrowed, noticing what I had ordered.

"It's a buckwheat crepe with mascarpone cheese, strawberries, pecans, and honey," I relayed.

Still no response.

It was like talking to a wall.

I cut into the crepe, giving him a hopeful look as I offered. "Want some?" I had to comment. "These already look much better than the ones in that diner near West 2nd and definitely better than that place by the south highway."

And he gave me an incredulous look.

Yes. I pursed my lips, trying to answer his unspoken question. *Ask me. The answer is yes.*

But he just looked away again, his eyes still distant.

I couldn't even blame him. From the start, I'd barely even let him know what I felt. Maybe it was time to give him the answers to all the questions I had just avoided.

"Yes," I declared. "When you asked if I felt that on the roof deck—yes, Lachlan, I felt that. No, it wasn't just you. I fell for you too. I'm pretty sure I couldn't have avoided it if I tried. And I agree, it *was* perfect."

I peered at his face, tipping forward. "Look, I know the last time I asked you for one last chance it was for Wanda and she totally blew it. But I'm asking now. For me. Would you give me one last chance? Please?"

I was already grimacing, already mocking myself since I wasn't betting the odds were in my favor.

He seemed to stiffen in his seat and stared at me for a long time before responding.

"I already have a girlfriend."

That statement stabbed my chest.

"Oh." I dropped my gaze to the table and I wanted to kick myself. *Ashleigh, you idiot. Of course,* he would have a new girl-friend by now.

Heat suffused my face as I should have clearly led with that question before I'd said all those stupid, pointless, em-barrassing, too-late things.

"She's really nice," Lachlan decided to share.

"Of course." I bobbed my head in vague agreement.

"So nice, in fact, that some people take advantage of that. Even bullies and stalkers." He tilted his head to go on. "But I've seen her stubborn side too. When she knows she's right, she *will* fight you. She taught me the difference between having confidence and being a total jack-ass."

I furrowed my eyebrows once I took in what he was actually saying. What? Was he talking about...?

"And we have so much in common. I don't think I'll enjoy troubleshooting computers or architectural tours again if I'm not with her."

I raised my eyes back to his in wonder but also almost in nervous dread as I couldn't possibly be hearing him right.

"And...she's very pretty." A corner of his mouth turned up. "Especially right now when she's looking at me like that."

I took a deep, shaky breath, needing to blink back an overwhelming wave of emotion.

"And I haven't stopped thinking about wanting to kiss her again since Christmas."

My heart pounded in my chest again and I couldn't bite back my smile in grateful relief, in bittersweet joy and anticipation.

His smile widened. "And she loves marshmallows."

That made me laugh.

Lachlan's gaze dropped to my hand on the table rested beside my plate and leaned forward ever so slightly to move his hand as though to touch mine.

But before he could, the swinging café door slammed shut again as if to announce the arrival of the waitress.

I jumped in my seat, backing away.

The girl came around to swap Lachlan's service number with his plate of food.

"Thank you," he called out to her retreating back.

I examined his plate. He had ordered some type of sweet crepe with pear, hot chocolate sauce, vanilla ice cream, and whipped cream on the side. "That looks great. What is that crepe called?"

After a beat, he replied, "Poire Belle."

His deep voice taking on that slight French accent sent a shiver running up my spine and I swallowed hard, resisting the urge to bite my lip.

"Looks good..." My gaze was still stuck on his mouth—which I maintained was totally his fault for bringing it up.

Looking adorably almost shy, Lachlan bent his head over his plate, biting his own lip.

I had to clear my throat, averting my gaze. I was sure my cheeks were red too but I was unable to tamp down my smile.

Lachlan gingerly sliced a piece of his crepe and when he held his fork out to me, that heavy burden was lifted off my chest. "You'll want to try this."

Absolutely tingling everywhere, I chewed on the mouthful, nodding in near bliss. "Mm. Is this the one you'd been looking for?"

And when Lachlan looked up and met my gaze again, his eyes were full of meaning with only a hint of that gorgeous smile on his face.

My own smile widened.

"Looks like a yes."

***

2I

Epilogue

Next Christmas

"Gosh, it's cold out there," I remarked as soon as Stella opened the door for me.

"'Tis the season." She smiled wide, gesturing me into their apartment foyer and pointing me to the coat rack. "Although can I just say on behalf of the group? We're very glad there hasn't been much whining from you about being stuck at school this Christmas."

I just laughed.

Yes. The weather gods were at it again.

Like an exact repeat of last year, I had been snowed in for the holidays.

But this year, I didn't mind.

And as I marveled up at the classic chandelier above the grand staircase, I couldn't help but think that this year's

Boxing Day Charity Gala was even more glittering and fabulous than the last.

"You can wait in the library if you want," Stella suggested as I hung up my coat.

I nodded, letting her bustle away to deal with some more party business as I turned right.

The library was a lush, brightly lit room, accentuated with the floor-to-ceiling pine bookshelves, walls and surfaces adorned with period artwork and decorative hurricane lamps.

I approached the window, smiling to myself as I peeked past the velvet curtain to watch the snow falling.

Outside, people bundled up in thick jackets and mittens walked past, gazing up in wonder at the building that must look almost magical glowing amidst the dark night.

I couldn't help a soft sigh.

A certain someone had been right yet again as despite getting off to a rocky start, this past year had been truly the absolute best ever.

The world went dark as warm hands covered my eyes from behind.

But I merely broke a knowing smile, not pulling away but instead leaning back against his tall frame. "Took you long enough."

Lachlan's deep voice rumbled from behind my ear. "It's not even midnight yet, Cinderella." He dropped his hands to my shoulders, bending his head to nuzzle my neck.

I shivered, turning to face him. "You know that tickles." I gave him an appreciative once-over in his suit jacket and open-collar shirt.

He chuckled at my appraisal. "Alright, settle down."

That made me crack up laughing and I playfully punched the sleeve of his tux.

But I had taken great pains to get ready for tonight as well. Little black dress and heels were definitely not normally part of my clothing repertoire.

I struck a little pose for him. "Well?"

Lachlan took a slow, deep breath as he panned his gaze from the bottom of my shoes all the way up to the top of my updo-styled hair.

When he met my gaze again, his gray eyes were already filled with such intensity and heat that my cheeks reddened, half self-consciously, half in pleasure.

He leaned closer for a moment. "You look perfect." Then he held his arm out for me with that now-familiar, disarming smile.

"Thank you."

We followed the canape guy up the stairs and across the grand salon so we could swipe some arancini rice balls. We ended up near the Christmas tree that was even bigger than last year's.

I spotted Mr. Hoffman decked out in a fancy maroon tuxedo, a glass of wine in hand, entertaining some guests. He happened to notice us and turned with a greeting.

"Ashleigh, I'm so glad you could attend our event this year. And this must be..." he trailed off, narrowing his eyes, not recognizing him.

Lachlan broke a polite smile anyway as he supplied again, "Lachlan."

"Ah, you must be Ashleigh's boyfriend," Mr. Hoffman drawled, gesturing a small nod of approval.

Lachlan's smile widened. "Yes, I am."

Honestly, I never tired of hearing it myself.

As we took a turn around the room and headed back toward the archway near the hearth, I spotted Stella and Pete mingling by the buffet and gave them a brief wave.

I tugged on Lachlan's hand to head over to them but skidded to a stop as I almost ran into Spencer who had popped out from behind the coat racks, his hair a bit mussed.

"Whoa," he mumbled, blinking at Lachlan and me in surprise.

"Uh, hey, Spencer." I gave him an odd look. "Are you okay in there?"

"Uh." He darted his gaze furtively around us as if trying to be discreet. "Hey, Lachlan and Ashleigh," he spoke out loud. "Glad you guys could make it tonight."

I met Lachlan's curious gaze for a moment before a dainty hand shot through the hanging coats to grasp Spencer's lapel and pull him back behind them.

My eyes widened in wonder as I thought I caught the sneaky Cheshire cat grin and sparkling green eyes of one Wanda Meyers from behind the dark tuxes before the gap closed, swallowing Spencer within it.

And my shoulders shook in mirth.

Way to go, Spencer.

Lachlan hadn't noticed. "Is he okay in there?" His eyebrows were furrowed in concern.

"Oh, I'm guessing he's quite alright in there." I bit back my chuckle.

Lachlan slid his arm around my waist to pull me closer.

"Look." He pointed up to the archway where a particular green leafy sprig had been hung.

We had both been here earlier today pitching in to help as usual, as per the newly established tradition and I gave him a suspicious look. "Did you put that there?"

Lachlan merely grinned, gazing down at me as though he couldn't get enough of how I looked. He pulled me close, cupping my face between his hands.

I stared up at the lights twinkling in his brilliant gray eyes, unable to believe how content I felt right at this moment.

I couldn't help an elated smile. "Merry Christmas."

Lachlan leaned over to kiss me. "I love you."

***

Don't miss a happy ending!

SARA BREAKER lives in New Zealand with her husband and two kids. She writes offbeat, quirky romance. Simple, sweet stories and epic happy endings.

Suburban mum by day and author by night, she loves to live vicariously through her characters. They don't have to vacuum all day long and are always guaranteed happy endings, no matter how melodramatic she writes them.

She likes binge-watching TV shows and reading books that take you through the requisite ups and downs of a good story, breaks your heart, puts it back together, bam! happy ending—but then still have enough time to wash the dishes after.

Subscribe to her mailing list and get a FREE e-book!

https://subscribe.breakerworlds.com/romance

Other Titles by Sara Breaker

Young Adult Sweet Romance
Just an Alternate
Change of Mind
That's So Sweet: Campus Players

New Adult Sweet Romance
Insert Happy Ending

Hale Valley Sweet Romance series
Switch on Christmas (a prequel novella)
Crushing on You

Sneak Peek

CHANGE OF MIND

School president Allie and popular jock Troy have been the best of enemies since the beginning of time. But things change...

* * *

Troy swung into the door to his Physics class in a casual non-hurried manner, nodding his head to some beat, scanning the chairs nonchalantly to find a place to park. He stopped short and tilted his head slightly to check if he wasn't seeing things.

The only seat left was beside none other than the infamous Allie Alberts.

Troy groaned inwardly. Normally, he'd never pass up the opportunity to poke more fun at her, but there was something weird going on with her lately, and he didn't wanna be around when she finally popped. Unfortunately, since he had arrived late, there wasn't any other option.

Table #6 was right in front of the teacher's desk, the kind only brave souls dared to occupy. Troy couldn't help but shake his head and think that it was incredibly typical of Allie to have chosen that seat. *Teacher's pet*, he thought to himself and only then realized that Allie shouldn't be in this class in the first place.

Allie's dismay was apparent the moment she met his gaze and worsened the moment she realized where he was headed.

"Hey Al," Troy greeted with an all-conceited smirk as he slid into the seat beside her. "Kick you out of Advanced Physics, did they?"

She returned his smirk sarcastically but didn't give him the satisfaction of an answer. Instead, she turned no-nonsensically back to writing down today's chapters in her notebook even as the course professor, Mr. Wieners, had apparently left the room for a while and wasn't anywhere in sight.

Troy leaned back in his seat, shaking his head again in ridicule. "Look at you, the teacher's not even in the room yet and you're already busy," he observed. "Gossip, comb your hair, doodle some guy's name in your notebook—you know, stuff girls do."

When Allie still didn't respond to his baiting, Troy grinned self-assuredly. "Fine," he raised his hands in resignation. "Wouldn't want your awesome bodyguard to come crashing down the door to beat me up with his Above Average I.Q., would I?" he teased of Caden.

Allie rolled her eyes sky high, not looking at him. *Sooo* creative. "A *special student* could do that," she replied wryly, not really intending to say it out loud but not really caring either way.

Troy's eyebrow quirked in surprise. "So the rumors *are* true," he remarked. "A nerd's bite is worse than its bark after all."

Allie didn't bother to stop to point out the many errors in his logic but instead regarded him with a business-like tone. "Look, Williams," she said. "I'm not really here to pretend I know you exist so I'd appreciate you not talking to me altogether, okay? You can mind your own business—whatever it is," she interjected. "—and I'll mind mine, is that clear?" she prompted with a fake condescending smile and a nod.

He gave her a strange look of ridicule before shaking his head, leaning forward on the table on his elbows. "Superiority complex, thy name is Allie Alberts," he muttered under his breath.

Allie heard him of course. "Huh, I thought he was seated next to me," she quipped just as Wieners returned, walking into the room as half the class slightly sat up in alert, such that Troy was unable to retort in his defense or in disbelief.

***

Enjoyed the preview? **Change of Mind** is also available to purchase at your favorite bookstore.

Sneak Peek

Can you handle a bit more steam? Try this quirky, offbeat New Adult/Contemporary Romance **When They Do** by Sara Bellcamp.

WHEN THEY DO

Alex Keaton is the hottest playboy on the West Coast, living the carefree single life. That is until his best friend decides to get married. And he finds himself chasing after the absolute last girl he would have ever imagined.

***

I was getting some drink refills for me and my date (which was code for flirting with the hot female bartender) when Janice found me at the bar.

"Hey," I greeted over the noise of the party. "Tyler here yet?"

Janice yelled in my ear. "He's on his way," she said. "He's picking up Claire from some law school alumni event. Where's Candace?"

"Charmaine," I corrected.

"Oh, so you do bother to know their names?" Janice mused.

I had to laugh. "Why do you always underestimate me?"

I asked her. "I can be a perfectly decent gentleman when I want to be."

She wiggled her eyebrows in agreement. "Yeah," she said wryly. "I can see that from your unnecessary tipping at an open bar—oh, finally!" she exclaimed, starting to wave both hands as if to get someone's attention from across the way. "Ty!" she called out.

And when I glanced over, I had to blink myself out of a startle. Tyler was making his way up to the pool area where we were. But my eyes had snapped straight to Claire who was right behind him.

She looked jaw-dropping hot!

She was wearing a low-cut snug little white number and her light brown hair was down her shoulders, wavy and tousled.

"Damn girl, you lookin' fine tonight," Janice commented, giving Claire an appraising look as she and Tyler approached us.

Claire gave her a deadpan look before stealing her drink. "Is that alcohol? Great." And she chugged it down quickly.

Janice's forehead creased. "Something wrong, sweetie?"

"No, no, just busy," Claire dismissed quickly. "Some of the senior partners just decided to throw this case referral down the ranks, and between that and dealing with the interns—"

I wasn't listening to the conversation but I was still staring at Claire. I would never have imagined that that body had been hiding under her usual three-piece business casual attire. Tyler had to elbow me to snap out of it.

He shot me a strange look. "Bro, you checkin' out Claire?"

"What? No," I replied quickly, instinctively, before I

stopped short. "I mean, yes. Hell yes," I amended, figuring there was no shame in admitting it.

"She does look different tonight, doesn't she?" Tyler commented.

"Different," I echoed. That was an understatement.

"Have you seen Marco yet?" he asked me.

"Oh, uh." I blinked a few times to clear my head. "Not yet actually." I panned my gaze around the crowd and spotted Nina quickly. She was wearing a shiny silver dress so it was easy to spot her. "There's Nina though. I bet if you stand close to her long enough, Marco will turn up," I remarked with a bit of sarcasm.

"Come on, Jan." Tyler took Janice's hand to pull her along in pursuit of Marco and/or Nina, leaving Claire standing beside me.

She didn't say anything. She wasn't even looking at me. But she took one of the glasses I was holding and drained it quickly. I had to grin. "I see time away from Marco is agreeing with you," I commented, giving her look another once-over.

"Oh my god." Claire shot me an annoyed look. "Would you just shut up? I don't want to talk about it."

"Jeez, someone's having a really bad day," I noted passively, then offered the other glass of wine I had to her. "My offer still stands, you know," I said with another grin. "Whenever you want to get that palette cleansed."

Naturally, I had seen Claire's look of scorn before but it was particularly prickly tonight. "It's that fast, is it?" she cut in, before declaring. "Just because Marco's got a new girlfriend doesn't mean you're suddenly allowed to hit on me."

Just then, I noticed Claire's gaze distract somewhere and I looked up to see what it was.

Tyler and Janice had found Marco and Nina. Marco, inexplicably, was also wearing a shiny silver shirt for tonight's party.

I was about to snicker and remark something insulting about matching couple outfits to Claire, but before I could say anything, Claire grabbed my second glass of wine, chugged it down quickly, then whirled around to walk away.

I tried to see where she went but she was quickly swallowed up by the party crowd.

***

Enjoyed the preview? **When They Do** is also available to purchase at your favorite bookstore.

9 780473 598617